The Facttracker

JASON CARTER EATON

The Facttracker

Illustrations by Pascale Constantin

HarperCollins*Publishers*

Library of Congress Cataloging-in-Publication Data is available.

ISBN 978-0-06-056434-6 (trade bdg.)

ISBN 978-0-06-056435-3 (lib. bdg.)

Typography by Larissa Lawrynenko

1 2 3 4 5 6 7 8 9 10

❖

First Edition

For my unbelievably amazing wife, Lisa.
Because ever since the chicken sukiyaki sandwich
I knew that you truly appreciated a good lie . . .
but only if it was really good.

Acknowledgments
I'd like to thank Mom, Dad and Nicole for their creative support, Milo for his love and cuteness, Tanya for all her guidance and direction, Phoebe for her keen and limitless editing, Pascale for her brilliant artwork, Ian for his friendship and schtick, Geppner for his geppnerosity, Sacks for teaching me the ancient Tibetan art of reverse ironic paradoxical sarcasm, Todd for inventing a new computer that auto-writes novels for you whilst gently massaging your feet and whispering "life is water" over and over, Rob and Sheryl for plugging the computer in, Cindy for informing me that a giant hula-hooping ninja space-robot was trying to steal my new computer, Parnell and Marinoff for helping me defeat the space-robot with the power of love and an even bigger robot, Grant for defending me before the intergalactic tribunal, Neal for testifying on my behalf, Riaz for taking that laser-blowdart for me on the courthouse steps, and Angela for clearing my good name before the totally unfair and biased Martian press (the space-robot clearly started it!).

CONTENTS

CHAPTER 1

Everyone Loves a Good Explosion

A FICTITIOUS FRIEND OF MINE once told me, "Everyone loves a good explosion." Sadly, he told this to me just moments before he himself exploded, but it was good advice nonetheless.

So let's begin with an explosion.

There was a sound—not quite a *ka-boom*, but not quite a *ker-pow* either. More like a *ka-blooey*. Then there were the flames—deep yellow, furious red, electric blue, and, of course, lots and lots of orange. And let's not forget about the heat—like a thousand suns crammed into a pizza oven wearing a giant wool sweater. And finally the debris—

1

first came the metal, all twisted and glowing. Then the bits of plastic, which had melted into globs of sticky, scalding goop. And lastly the facts, **millions of them**, shooting off into the far corners of the sky like a tremendous meteor shower, except in reverse.

I'll pause now, since I'm sure you're saying, "Wait. Facts? Did you say . . . facts?"

To which I say, "Yes, facts."

Which of course leads to the logical next question: What could possibly blow up that would send *facts* into the sky?

Well, you'll have to wait for that. There's a whole book to get through here, and you don't want to know everything in the first chapter. I mean, you haven't even heard about the Facttracker or the just small enough boy.

But wasn't the explosion cool?

CHAPTER 2

*The Facttracker and the Just Small Enough
Boy Are Introduced, but Then Things
Quickly Get* COMPLICATED

IN THE TOWN OF TRAÄKERFAXX, at the foot of the hill that led up to the Facttracker, lived a very sad and lonely boy who was so small that he was almost too small. But not quite. He was just small enough. And that was exactly how he was known, as the just small enough boy. Now, in order to understand the just small enough boy, you have to understand Traäkerfaxx. And in order to understand Traäkerfaxx, you have to understand the Facttracker.

This is where things get complicated.

Let's begin with the Facttracker. He's the man who finds, collects, and keeps track of the world's facts. Not just some of them, but *all* of them. Facts like the population of Nebraska (two million), and the temperature of a healthy human person (98.6°F), and even the exact number of facts tracked since facttrackers began tracking facts, which is a very large number indeed, since facttrackers have been tracking facts since the dawn of man, give or take a few years. There has always been one facttracker at any given time, and he has always spent his entire life at the top of the hill in Traäkerfaxx, tracking facts.

Quick, what's the population of Nebraska? If you said two million, you're wrong. It's one million nine hundred ninety-nine thousand nine hundred ninety-seven. Three people just moved away because they all got jobs in a Chinese tea bag factory. Which shows just how quickly facts can change and just how much work the Facttracker must have.

You've never heard of a facttracker? Well, that's because you don't live in Traäkerfaxx. If you did, you'd know that every fact that you've ever heard or read was originally discovered by the Facttracker and then sold by the people of Traäkerfaxx to whoever wanted it.

In fact, Traäkerfaxx is the facttracking capital

of the world. There's even a big wooden sign when you enter the town that reads:

TRAÄKERFAXX: A SWELL PLACE TO TRACK FACTS

The just small enough boy knew that sign very well. It was the first thing he saw every morning when he woke up and the last thing he saw before he went to bed.

That's because he lived under it.

Now, surely you must be saying, "Waitaminute! You can't fit a house under a sign! Just how big is this sign anyway?" Good point. But it's not that the sign was so very big; it's that the house was so very small. You see, the just small enough boy lived in a doghouse. A doghouse under a town sign.

As you can imagine, it wasn't a very glamorous life.

The doghouse had belonged to the town mayor, who, in an uncharacteristic fit of generosity, donated it to the just small enough boy after his

dog had run away to seek a more glamorous life. As far as doghouses go, it wasn't particularly bad. There were four solid walls, a nice cathedral ceiling, and above the door, in faded gold letters, was the word GLAMOROUS, which coincidentally had been the mayor's dog's name.

Now, I'm sure you're saying, "Waitaminute!

How could his parents let him live in a doghouse? That's monstrous!" True. But let's be honest—when you don't even have a proper name, how can you expect to have a proper house?

Yes, now I'm sure you're saying, "Well, why doesn't he have a proper name?"

Good question. And there's a good answer for it too.

*A Just Small Enough Chapter About
the Just Small Enough Story of
the Just Small Enough Boy*

As I MENTIONED EARLIER, after the Facttracker tracks a fact, it is then shipped by the townspeople to whoever wants to buy that particular fact. Years ago, when the just small enough boy was born, his facts were paid for by his parents, who naturally wanted to know all about their new son. They were so excited to learn about him that they took the child and drove all the way to Traäkerfaxx rather than wait for the facts to be shipped to them. But when they went to pick the facts up at the Factory, something terrible happened.

Something horribly terrible.

Now, the just small enough boy's parents were reasonably bright people. In fact, for people of their age and size, they had an awful lot of facts crammed into their heads. But there were still three facts in particular that they didn't have:

@ That the then half-completed Factory was still under construction and so had many gigantic unfinished holes in its structure.

@ That there were an awfully large number of facts about the boy, and so rather than being stuck in a crate they were wrapped up in a great big bundle, a fact bundle, which was stored at the top of the Factory and tied down with a knot of string.

🍴 That the Facttracker was hungry and so had gone out for some lunch.

The parents of course knew none of this. If they had known, I'm certain they would not have knocked quite so forcefully on the Factory door. But sadly, that's exactly what they did.

And that's when the horribly terrible thing happened.

The vibration of the knock loosened the knot holding the fact bundle in place. The large and heavy fact bundle slipped away, rolled straight through a giant hole in the Factory wall, and landed square on the boy's unsuspecting parents with a noise that sounded somewhere between *squish* and *squash*. His parents weren't killed—that would have been simply awful—but they *were* stuck to the tumbling bundle like two tiny biscuit crumbs on a wet sponge. The bundle paused just long enough for the two plastered parents to shout out, "**Look after our boy!**" and then continued rolling down the hill and out of Traäkerfaxx forever.

The poor child was left without any facts about himself and, far worse, without any parents.

Only one tiny stray fact was ever recovered: that the boy was neither too small nor not small enough. And so from that moment on he was known to everyone who knew him, which was everyone in Traäkerfaxx, as the just small enough boy.

The just small enough boy was taken care of by the good people of Traäkerfaxx, which wasn't such a good thing since "good people" is really just an expression. Like "a bad egg," or "ants in my pants," or "a bad egg in my pants," which is a popular expression in Traäkerfaxx. Now, that's not to say the Traäkerfaxxians were bad people. They just never felt bad about being mean to the just small enough boy because they didn't really know anything about him.

It's extremely easy to be mean to people you don't really know.

"If I knew who he was, perhaps I wouldn't order him around so much," the mayor would say. "But I don't know *anything* about him. No one does. Sure, he could be a king. But on the other hand, he could also be a filthy little ragamuffin with tuna fish for brains and brown paper bags for shoes. I guess I'll just have to take that chance. Just small enough boy! Get my bullfrog a tuna fish sandwich!"

It was a hard life, and the just small enough boy often wondered, in the brief moments when he wasn't being ordered around, how different his life would be if he ever found out who he was.

Each morning he would wake up before everyone else and quietly roam through Traäkerfaxx, picking up whatever odd facts he could find lying about. Usually all he found were small, measly scraps of facts, like that the biggest ingredient in fried chicken is chicken. Every now and then he would come across a really juicy fact that accidentally fell off someone's cart, like that the longest named place in America is Lake Chargoggagoggmanchaugagoggchaubunagungamaug in Massachusetts.

Over time the just small enough boy became a bit of a fact collector and even kept his favorite ones taped to the walls of his doghouse. He found facts about nearly every single thing you could think of. But, disappointingly, he never came across a single fact about himself or, even more disappointingly, his parents.

It was all very disappointing.

Until the day a very peculiar thing happened. The just small enough boy was passing by the Factory when he heard a distant whistle. He couldn't be sure, but it sounded as if it had come from the Factory's top floor. Squinting, he looked up and saw a tiny white speck pop out of the window. It circled the Factory several times as it wound its way down to the ground. As it got closer and closer, the just small enough boy realized what it was—a paper airplane. The airplane glided once more around the tower, did a fancy loop the loop, and then landed right at his feet.

The just small enough boy picked it up and unfolded it. Across the middle of the paper, in gently written words, was one simple sentence: "I'm looking for your facts too."

The just small enough boy looked back up at the top floor of the Factory, but all he could see was a small blur pass by the window. Still, there was no doubt that this was a message and little doubt that the message was meant for him. There was even less doubt when he turned the paper over and noticed that there was a tiny little fact taped to it. He peeled it off and read it:

"The boy's father's favorite food is chicken Parmesan."

A fact about his parents! It was a spot of light in the just small enough boy's dark and dismal existence. He ran home and taped it to the wall of his doghouse, right above his bed.

The next day a second paper airplane popped out of the window, proclaiming,

"Thought I saw your fact bundle in the ocean. Turned out to be a whale. Will keep looking."

And taped to the back was a fact about the just small enough boy's mother (she once had a dog named Schnoodle that was half schnauzer, half poodle).

Another day, another plane.

"Adding more veriscopes to Factory. Will see if this helps."

The just small enough boy had no idea what a

veriscope was, but he was happy that the Facttracker was adding more of them. And he was even happier for the new fact about his parents (they were married on Halloween).

Of course the just small enough boy had no way of responding (it's extremely difficult to glide a paper airplane *up* a tower), but he was more than content for the correspondence, even if it was only one way.

This went on for years. The Facttracker sent notes down whenever he had a new idea or plan, and the just small enough boy read them and got excited. Eventually the walls of his doghouse were completely covered with the facts about his parents. But neither his fact bundle nor his parents were ever found.

And that's it.

Now, surely you must be saying, "That's it? How can that be it? That can't be it. What about his parents? Didn't he ever look for them? Didn't he ever meet the Facttracker?"

Those are all very good questions. And the answer is yes. And by "yes" I mean "yes, that's it." Sorry, but it's hard to fit everything into a just small enough chapter.

Sorry to Do This, but There's a Lot of
Information in This Book, and I Need to Make Sure
You're Paying Attention

POP QUIZ! What's the population of
Nebraska? If you said one million nine
hundred ninety-nine thousand nine hundred ninety-seven, you're wrong. It's one million
nine hundred ninety-nine thousand nine hundred ninety-*eight*. A very old man just moved
there to observe a very old oak tree. So far it seems
to be all he'd hoped it would be.

CHAPTER 3

I Bet You Forgot All About the Explosion.
Didn't You? You Didn't? Well That's Good, Because
We're Getting Closer to It

THE MORNING OF THE explosion was a morning like any other, except that it was soon to be followed by an explosion. The just small enough boy woke up to the sound of the mayor's voice.

"Just small enough boy," he called, banging frantically on the roof of the doghouse, "wake up! There's been an emergency!"

The just small enough boy rubbed his eyes quickly, leaped out of bed, and threw open the door. He was greeted by a panting and sweating mayor, who appeared to have something green and limp in his arms.

"What's wrong?" the just small enough boy asked in a panic-stricken voice.

The mayor held up the limp green object. "My bullfrog. He's thirsty. Maybe even dehydrated. I don't know. I'm no expert on bullfrogs. But you should get him a glass of warm lime juice anyway."

The bullfrog croaked indifferently.

The just small enough boy sighed and rolled his eyes. "I really don't think bullfrogs drink warm lime juice," he said.

The mayor's eyes went wide with indignation, and he puffed himself up. "Are *you* an expert on bullfrogs?" he demanded. "Because I don't think you are. No, I don't recall ever seeing *that* fact about you. And since neither of us is a bullfrog expert, then it stands to reason that my idea, which was said first, is right."

The just small enough boy shuffled uneasily and tried to sound as casual as possible, which of course sounded even more uncasual than if he hadn't tried altering the casualness at all.

"Maybe I could go see if the Facttracker has any facts about bullfrogs . . ."

"Oh, you'd love that, wouldn't you, just small enough boy? Some facts about bullfrogs and, what, maybe some *other* things? Maybe some things about *you*? That's very selfish, just small enough boy. You're selfish. Don't think I don't know about your little note passing with the Facttracker. I know all about it, and you need to stop wasting the Facttracker's time. I see you looking up at the Factory every day, looking up and wanting to go in. What are you looking for anyway, just small enough boy? Who you are? You're the just small enough boy, and that should be enough." He poked the just small enough boy with the bullfrog. "Now go get some warm lime juice for my dehydrated bullfrog!"

The bullfrog croaked phlegmatically, and the just small enough boy trudged off, grumbling. He wasn't particularly upset about the lime juice—a good portion of *every* day was spent fetching things for the mayor and his bullfrog—but he was annoyed with himself for having mentioned the Facttracker. Now the mayor would be watching him, and the just small enough boy knew that he probably wouldn't have another opportunity to check for a paper airplane until the evening.

It had been over a month since the last paper airplane—a hastily written note saying simply, "Big news soon"—and the just small enough boy was beginning to get worried. In fact, all sorts of awful thoughts were beginning to take root in his mind. *Maybe the Facttracker has given up. Maybe my facts never existed. Maybe he found my parents, but they don't want me anymore.*

The just small enough boy sneaked one quick glance up at the Factory and then set off to find some warm lime juice.

Far larger than the paltry, half-finished Factory that the just small enough boy's parents had seen, the modern-day Factory was an enormous copper tower that stretched a half mile up into the sky. Located in the center of Traäkerfaxx, it looked sort of like a gigantic metal tree, except that where there would normally be branches, long, twisty telescopes poked out in every conceivable direction. It was a beautiful sight, though, like most beautiful sights in most towns, few people in Traäkerfaxx ever bothered to look at it.

On sunny days, when he managed to finish all the mayor's tasks (or avoid him entirely), the just small enough boy would lie in the grass at the bottom of the Factory and stare straight up in hope of catching a glimpse of a paper airplane or, better yet, the Facttracker. But a half mile is a long distance, and though the just small enough boy occasionally thought he saw a tiny gray blur scuttle past a window, what the Facttracker was doing inside the Factory remained a mystery.

Now, you should know, it wasn't just a mystery to the just small enough boy. It was a mystery to *everyone* in Traäkerfaxx. It had, in fact, been years since anyone had even laid eyes on the Facttracker. The accident with the just small enough boy's parents had shut down production for several days and cost the town a great deal of money. And so, to prevent that from ever happening again, the mayor ordered that the Factory doors be shut tight. That may have been all fine and good for the Traäkerfaxxians but made for a very lonely Facttracker.

At least that's my theory. I haven't seen him in a while either.

CHAPTER 4

We're Almost at the Explosion. I Promise

THE AFTERNOON OF THE explosion was an afternoon like any other, except that it was even closer to the explosion than the morning of the explosion had been.

The just small enough boy spent most of the afternoon running errands for the mayor and his bullfrog. After fetching the warm lime juice, he was told to fetch some cold lime juice to wash it down. Then he was told to fetch some whole limes. Then to pick up some dental floss to help the bullfrog get the lime pulp out of his teeth. And finally he was sent off to find a copy of *Bullfrog Monthly*, which the mayor said was his bullfrog's favorite magazine.

It had been a long, exhausting day, especially since there was no such thing as *Bullfrog Monthly*, and the just small enough boy wanted nothing more than to lie in the grass and stare up at the Factory. The sun was just beginning to set, so he quickened his pace. As much as he enjoyed looking at the Factory during the day, there was nothing he loved more than watching the Factory at dusk. In those brief moments before the Facttracker turned off the equipment and went to bed, the top floor of the Factory lit up like a torch against the darkening sky. The just small enough boy had noticed with growing enthusiasm that the lights had been getting brighter and brighter over the last several weeks, and he was anxious to see how much brighter it was today. It had been fiercely bright the night before, and he felt certain that it couldn't get much brighter without eliminating dusk altogether.

The just small enough boy made his way quickly through the twisty cobblestone streets, watching anxiously as his shadow grew longer and longer. Finally, he turned onto Fact Sheet Street, which was the main street in Traäkerfaxx, located right in the heart of the fact district. At the very end of the street was a large triangular building, the Traäkerfaxx Fact Sales and Distribution Office. This was where the majority of the townspeople spent their days, selling the countless facts that the Facttracker tracked for them.

The just small enough boy breathed a sigh of relief.

Traäkerfaxx, you see, was essentially a large ring of streets and houses and shops all surrounding a great big field in the middle. There were only four things in this field: the hill; the Factory, built at the top of the hill; and the just small enough boy's doghouse, built under the town sign at the bottom of the hill. The Traäkerfaxx Fact Sales and Distribution Office was the last building in the maze of cobblestone streets, and the just small enough boy knew whenever he saw it that he was nearly out of the maze and would soon be in the open field.

As he passed by he heard the familiar sound of the facts being shot down the pneumatic tube by the Facttracker: *THOONK . . . THOONK . . . THOONK!*

This was punctuated by the sales pitches piping out through the open windows.

"Yes indeed, madam! A fact about pinwheels?

We have several of those in stock."

"Would you like those nose hair facts shipped overnight or regular delivery?"

The just small enough boy couldn't help feeling a pang of jealousy for all the people getting the facts they wanted. It seemed grossly unfair to him that trivial facts about pinwheels and nose hair were readily available to anyone who asked for them, but his own personal facts, which he would cherish like the most precious treasure, were nowhere to be found.

Without even realizing what he was doing, he quietly moved under the window and raised his ears, hoping that perhaps through some twist of chance he might hear one of his facts mentioned. But after a few moments the voices inside stopped talking, and soon after, a great throng of Traäkerfaxxians came pouring out the front door. Their workday was officially over, which meant that the Facttracker had stopped dropping facts down from the Factory.

The just small enough boy stood there quietly, unnoticed, as the townspeople brushed past him. After about a minute the lights in the building went out, and the just small enough boy was all alone again.

He looked up at the sky and frowned. The sun had just dipped below the horizon, and the last hints of light were already faded. There was no point in running now; he knew that he was too late. By now the Facttracker would be descending the steps, and the lights would all be off.

"A miserable end to a lousy day," he mumbled to himself as he walked the last stretch, staring at the ground and absentmindedly kicking any discarded facts in his path. But as he approached the town center, he noticed that a crowd had gathered around the base of the hill leading up to the Factory.

"What's going on?" asked the just small enough boy.

"What a silly question," replied the mayor. "We're waiting."

"Oh," said the just small enough boy, looking at him. "Why?"

"Isn't it obvious?" said the mayor, pointing straight up.

The just small enough boy looked up. He could hardly believe his eyes. The entire top floor of the Factory was ablaze with light. Not only that, but the branchlike telescopes, which normally remained stationary, were now swaying back and forth rhythmically as though bobbing on some unseen breeze. It was a spectacular sight.

"The lights have never been on at night," said the just small enough boy.

"We know that, just small enough boy," said the mayor.

"Something must be wrong with the Facttracker," the just small enough boy said urgently. "Shouldn't someone check on him?"

"Oh, you'd love that, wouldn't you, just small enough boy?" barked the mayor. "Well, forget it! The Factory doors are locked! And do you know why they're locked? So that people like you can't distract the Facttracker. You distracted him years ago, and we lost a whole day of work from him. Which meant we lost a whole day of facts from him. Which meant we lost a whole day of income for us."

"But—"

"No, the only thing to do is wait."

"But what if it's an emergency?" said the just small enough boy. "What if the Facttracker's sick?"

"No. We wait," said the mayor. But just then the mayor had a thought that he simply couldn't keep to himself. "If the Facttracker is sick . . . then . . . then who's going to track our facts?" he asked.

A gasp ran through the townspeople.

"But we have to have facts!" exclaimed a man wearing red shoes. "I told my children that Traäkerfaxx is the facttracking capital of the world. What am I supposed to tell them now? Huh?"

"And I just told a lima bean farmer looking to spice up his life that I had some top-notch facts about turnips," added a woman in bell-bottom pants.

"I can't remember if potatoes are more popular than sweet potatoes," yelled a man with a green striped tie. "Or is it the other way around? I've got a real bad egg in my pants about this!"

The townspeople were in a state of panic. They had no idea what they would do if the Facttracker was indeed sick. But just then the mayor had another thought.

"Maybe the Facttracker has died."

CHAPTER 5

*The Answer to Whether the Facttracker Had in Fact
Died, and Also Some Other Things*

INSIDE THE FACTORY, unbeknownst to the townspeople, the Facttracker was far from dead. In
fact, he was very much alive. He was dancing.
He was dancing a Mexican Hat Dance. The
Facttracker was dancing a Mexican Hat Dance
because that was the only dance left. He had
already danced every other kind of dance there
was, from the Charleston to the Polka. He had
even danced the Funky Facttracker, a dance that
he had invented himself.

The Facttracker was dancing because he was
happy. And he was happy because he was celebrating.

He
was celebrat-
ing because
he was done
facttracking.

It had taken exactly fifty years. Fifty years of
sitting at his desk, in his constellation-print facttracker uniform, surrounded by tens of thousands
of hundreds of millions of instruments. Fifty long
years of dropping facts, like "Potatoes are still outselling sweet potatoes in Idaho," down a pneumatic tube to the anxiously waiting townspeople

below. And worst of all, fifty tremendously long years of going up and down a half mile of spiral steps.

Now that was all over. And the Facttracker was about as happy as any man had ever been.

Ah, but surely you must surely be saying, "Aren't there new facts each and every day? Isn't there a new fact every time something new appears? Like a baby. Or a loaf of bread. Or a baby loaf of bread with a baby inside who is eating a smaller loaf of bread. That's new. And it should have some new facts about it."

Well, you're absolutely right. But you'd be absolutely wrong if you think that the Facttracker hadn't thought of that already. I mean, he's the Facttracker; do you really think he's not going to know a simple thing like that? In fact, if there's one fact he *is* going to know, it would be that, because it's a fact about facts.

Remember all those tens of thousands of hundreds of millions of instruments? Well, he really used only about three or four of them. The rest of them were for the day the Factory could run on its own. And he had finally reached that day. That was why he was dancing. And that was why all the instruments were flashing and blinking.

It was a great day for the Facttracker. For you see, the Facttracker didn't particularly like facts.

Well, that's not exactly true. He appreciated them, and he had the greatest respect for their importance, and in a very deep emotional way he actually loved them. But after fifty years he was just a little tired of them.

This was not a particularly uncommon dilemma for a facttracker. It had happened to the Facttracker's father, and *his* father before him, and *his* father before even him. In fact, it had happened to every facttracker since the dawn of facttracking, which was essentially the dawn of man, give or take a few years.

Part of the reason was that facttracker training begins at a very early age. The present facttracker's apprenticeship began when he was only two, which meant that he never got to be a regular little boy, the kind of little boy who enjoyed playing in fields and flying kites and climbing trees. He wanted to do these things, but he couldn't. There were always facts that needed tracking.

And back in those days it was far, far worse. You see, there was no Factory; facttracking was a much more hands-on process. There were no buttons or knobs or any other kinds of complex instruments. His father had to go out and personally track each and every fact. Needless to say, he was able to find far fewer facts back then, which was why far fewer things were known. He never found the fact that a rocket ship could take you to the moon or the fact that computers could tell you all sorts of important information. He never even discovered the fact that ketchup makes hamburgers taste better. Back then everyone ate their hamburgers with tartar sauce, which was why hamburgers weren't very popular. They also made their tartar sauce out of toothpaste, which was why tartar sauce wasn't popular either.

Truth be told, the Facttracker's dad spent his entire career hoping he would one day have the time to play in a field or fly a kite or climb a tree. But it never seemed to happen. And so when the day finally came for him to retire, he called his son into his office, which was little more than a small wooden shack with facts strewn about everywhere, and sat him down.

"Son," he said, "I have tracked facts my whole life, but I can track them no more. You are the Facttracker now. But learn from my mistakes! Don't spend your life hunting for facts, one by one. Be smart. Modernize. And when you are done, do a dance for me. Do several dances. And end with a Mexican Hat Dance."

And with that he held out his clenched fists for his son and opened them one at a time. The right one contained a small glowing orb, a very rare seed of truth, to be precise, which is the thing at the heart of all facts. The left contained a teensy tiny little fact, his last and most prized: that a factory could be built to track facts for him.

Then he ran out giggling and climbed the first tree he found.

CHAPTER 6

*The Answer to a Question That Wasn't
Even Asked. And the Question Is This: What Were
the Townspeople Up To?*

BACK IN THE TOWN the townspeople were
getting nervous. They didn't know about
the dancing or the Factory's being self-
sufficient, and they certainly hadn't read the last
chapter. All they knew was that the Facttracker
had gone to the top of the Factory but hadn't come
down.

"Just small enough boy," whispered the mayor,
"go see if the Facttracker's dead."

This was a curious moment for the just small
enough boy. After years of staring up at the outside of the forbidden Factory, he was actually being
ordered to go in. And now, to his utter surprise and

34

amazement, he found himself a little scared. After all, the Factory was a great big mystery to him, and while oftentimes mysteries end up being fun and exciting, other times they end up horrible and terrifying. Especially when they involve a maybe-dead person. That's just the way mysteries are.

"By myself?" pleaded the just small enough boy.

"You'll see if the Facttracker's dead and you'll enjoy every second of it!" shouted a woman with a wart on a mole on her chin.

"Yeah, but don't enjoy the seconds *too* much, just small enough boy!" added a man with only one shoe on. "If they're *that* enjoyable, bring some seconds back for *us*."

The just small enough boy sighed and turned toward the Factory. He knew that for better or worse, this was the opportunity he'd been waiting for.

So he swallowed his fear and began walking to the Factory. As he made his way across the field, the just small enough boy heard the cries of the townspeople.

"Let us know what happens!" shouted a man in a scarf.

"Try to find out about that potato–sweet potato thing if you can!" said another man in another scarf.

"Remember to take your hat off. It's the polite thing to do!" said a man with a pencil-thin mustache and an all-white suit.

The mayor accompanied the just small enough boy up the hill. When they reached the Factory, he took out a large key and inserted it into the Factory's front door. The townspeople let out a collective *oooh* and then an *aaah* as the lock swirled, groaned, went *KA-KUNK*, and then clicked open.

Then, as the just small enough boy's hand, trembling with nervousness, reached out, they all hushed with equally nervous silence. The just small enough boy closed his eyes, stiffened his trembling hand, and turned the doorknob. The great copper door swung open, revealing the candlelit interior of the Factory. The mayor nudged the just small enough boy forward but was too nervous to say anything. The just small enough boy took a deep breath and stepped inside. He turned around to get some last-minute encouragement, but the mayor had slammed the door shut again and was already halfway down the hill.

The nervous townspeople nervously watched the Factory, nervously wondering what the just small enough boy would say when he came back and nervously wondering if he would ever come back at all. They waited, and waited, and waited, and waited, and waited, and waited, and waited, and waited. Actually, that's not really true. They didn't wait that last wait. I exaggerated.

But then, with no warning at all, there came from the top of the tower a town-shattering *kablooey*. None of the townspeople knew what happened. The mayor didn't know what happened. Even you don't know what happened. I know what happened, but I can hardly believe it.

Here is what happened.

CHAPTER 7

What Happened

WHEN THE MAYOR slammed the door, the force of it blew out all the candles in the room. And so the just small enough boy suddenly found himself all alone, in the forbidden and mysterious Factory, possibly with a dead fact-tracker, in the dark. He bit his lip, which was all he could do to keep from crying.

But after a few moments his eyes gradually adjusted to the dark, and he was soon able to notice that the room was slightly less dark in one direction. He made his way toward the light as carefully as he could, blindly feeling his way through the room with his outstretched hands. At one point he felt something sharp and pointy; at another he felt something soft and velvety. What these things were remained a mystery.

Eventually he reached the source of the light, which he now knew was a thin strip of space under another door. He slowly felt for the door-knob and then opened the door.

"O-o-o-oh!" said the just small enough boy in disbelief.

Before him stood a circular room so large and bright that it seemed impossible that it was made entirely of copper. And yet it was. The whole expanse—and it was quite expansive—was covered floor to ceiling in the metal. Now, you'd think that an all-metal room would feel cold and imper-sonal. But it was exactly the opposite. The moment the just small enough boy saw it he was filled with a warmth that he'd never felt before.

The room wasn't just one long sheet of copper. It was made up of thousands, perhaps even mil-lions, of strips—each a slightly different age, each a slightly different color. The whole thing looked like a bizarre patchwork quilt.

Amazed at the magnificence of the Factory, the just small enough boy walked in. He had never seen anything like it. Which was understandable since there *wasn't* anything like it.

But it was nothing compared with what he saw when he looked up: a spiral staircase that seemed to stretch upward to infinity.

The just small enough boy walked across the room to where the stairway started. Along the wall, at regular intervals, were peepholes that seemed to belong to the telescope branches he'd seen from the outside.

As he began his journey up the stairs, the just small enough boy tried looking through one of the telescopes. But no matter how much he squinted, all he could see was darting, blurry lines. After peeking through a few telescopes, he decided that either he was doing something wrong or they were broken.

Around and around and around he went, step by step, flight after endless flight. Time passed, but he had no idea how long. He was breathing hard, and cold beads of sweat dripped down the curves behind his just small enough ears. All he wanted to do was reach the top.

And just as he thought he couldn't go a single step farther, he suddenly heard a familiar skipping sound that seemed to him vaguely Mexican.

Rounding the final loop of stairs, he recognized the tune as a hat dance, and his eyes narrowed with curiosity. But what he saw next made his eyes shoot back open as wide as they could go and then a little wider.

For there, on the top floor of the Factory tower, stood a tall, graying, dignified man, beaming with delight, holding a tuna fish sandwich in his hand, and dancing around to the Mexican Hat Dance as tens of thousands of hundreds of millions of instruments blinked and flickered and flashed all around him.

The just small enough boy had no idea what to say.

But before he could think of something, the Facttracker stopped dancing and spun around, staring at him curiously. There was a moment's pause as each looked at the other, and then the Facttracker spoke.

"Hello," he said, smiling through the tuna fish sandwich, which was now in his mouth.

"Uh, hello," said the just small enough boy, managing a just small enough smile.

"Come in, come in! We meet at last!" said the Facttracker excitedly, spitting out the sandwich. "Please come in. We must discuss things. Yes, a discussion. A discussion, and then we can get to your facts. But please, let us not discuss facts yet. Anything but that. Cheese perhaps? Come in, come in. May I offer you a tuna fish sandwich? Please come in."

The just small enough boy was dumbstruck. He had so many questions for the Facttracker, questions that he had kept at the front of his brain for years. But the instant he saw this strange, animated man, he couldn't remember a single one of them.

"So," said the Facttracker eagerly, "what's your favorite cheese?"

"Um, American?" he answered after some thought.

"Hmm. Yes. Yes, I can see that. Good for grilled cheese sandwiches, nice in omelets. A fine cheese all around. I personally prefer Muenster. It just sounds funny. Muenster cheese. Say it with me. *Mmmmuenster* cheese."

"Muenster cheese," said the just small enough boy.

"Cracks me up every time," said the Facttracker, chuckling. "But let's not let cheese stand between us. I'll enjoy my cheese and you'll enjoy your cheese, and no one will be any the cheesier." The Facttracker did one last little round of hat dancing, wiped a spot of tuna from his chin, and sat down across from the just small enough boy.

"A fine conversation," he said, "just fine. I haven't had one of those in a long, long time." He took a deep, contented breath. "So," he said, "I assume you're curious about everything here. Do you have the blueprints?"

The just small enough boy looked confused. "What blueprints?" he asked.

"The one I wrote today's message on," said the Facttracker. "You know, telling you to come up."

"I didn't get any message from you today," said the just small enough boy. "I haven't for a while now. At least a month. I came because the townspeople were worried about you."

"Worried? But I've been sending your airplanes out every day. I sent you one just this morning on the blueprints to the Factory. You were supposed to show them to the mayor so he knew about the Factory and why you should be allowed up. I don't understand—"

The just small enough boy's eyes narrowed. "The mayor," he grumbled angrily. "He told me this morning that he knew all about the messages. He must have been intercepting them somehow."

43

"Well, no matter," said the Facttracker. "You made it here anyway."

"I was worried that—"

"That I'd given up?" asked the Facttracker. "Or forgotten all about you?" The just small enough boy nodded quietly. "Nothing could be further from the truth," said the Facttracker, "and the truth is what I specialize in. I've wanted to meet you for ages now, ever since the accident. You have no idea how terrible I've felt about it. Horribly terrible! I spent years looking for your fact bundle, but it proved near impossible to track—at least with ordinary means. Those facts had picked up a lot of momentum over the years, and the world's a very big place. Every now and then I would find one of your parents' facts, but no matter what I tried, I was always one step behind that darned bundle. Of course I gave you all of your parents' facts, but it's not the same as giving you your actual parents. I just couldn't meet you until I was able to return everything of yours that I'd lost."

"So you found them?" asked the just small enough boy excitedly. "You found my parents? You found my facts?"

"No, no, no," said the Facttracker equally excitedly. "Not yet. But I'm about to. That's what all this is for." He gestured around the room to the countless pieces of machinery that littered the walls. The just small enough boy stared in awe at the tens of thousands of hundreds of millions of flickering and flashing buttons, knobs, and levers.

"Today is a momentous day," continued the Facttracker. "Today the Factory will be able to track facts . . . without a facttracker. And not only that, but better too!" His eyes sparkled with wild exhilaration. "We'll be able to find out what's at the bottom of the ocean, or underneath the Himalayas, or at the end of the universe! There isn't a single fact that we won't be able to track now!" He sat down and then mused in a slightly quieter voice: "Oh, I suppose there will be some problems. Information just flooding in can be a little unnerving in its own way. And maybe it's better not to know *some* things. Mysteries make us tick more than just about anything else. Yes, things will change, certainly. But things always change, don't they?"

The just small enough boy, however, hardly heard him. He was completely transfixed by a great glass silo in the corner of the room. It was filled, top to bottom, with thousands upon thousands of facts.

"I've never seen so many facts," he said quietly.

"That's just today's haul," explained the Facttracker. "Go on, grab a few," he told the just small enough boy. "On the house." He lifted up the boy.

The just small enough boy closed his eyes, reached in, and snatched a handful of facts. Like a boy on his birthday, he quickly opened his hands up, pulled the facts out, and read them hungrily.

"'If you're ever lost, the North Star makes a perfect point of reference,' and 'If a month begins on a Sunday, it will have a Friday the thirteenth,' and 'Toenails grow four times more slowly than fingernails.'"

"Oooh. A very nice assortment," said the Facttracker, lowering him back down, "useful and interesting."

"I'll add them to my collection," said the just small enough boy, and stuffed them in his pants pocket. Then something else grabbed his attention: something quite peculiar, a tiny shiny golden object that looked like a miniature version of the Factory.

"What's this?" he asked, picking it up.

"Ah, I see you found the veriscope!" said the Facttracker, leaping over happily. "That's how facts are found. This little doohickey's been in my family for aeons. Every facttracker who's ever lived has used it. Me, my brother, my father, my father's father, my father's father's father, my father's father's father's . . . well, you get it. Anyway, with the Factory up and running on its own I suppose there's no need for it anymore. It's just another antique now. Want it?"

"What? Really? Are you serious?" asked the just small enough boy.

"Absolutely. Here, look," said the Facttracker, putting it gently to the just small enough boy's eye and adjusting it here and there with a skilled, delicate touch.

The just small enough boy gasped as the room changed around him. Gone were the instruments and buttons and walls and floor, and in their place were words—hazy, wispy words—that darted all around the room like wild billiard balls.

"I—I can see words," said the just small enough boy, squinting into the veriscope, "but I can't quite make them out."

"That's because you don't know what to look for," said the Facttracker. "Here, try pointing it at me. Now, don't look for anything in particular; just look at me as a whole. You don't want to lead the veriscope; you want to let the veriscope lead you."

The just small enough boy put his eye to the veriscope again. A moment later he saw the Facttracker not as a person but as a conglomeration of swirling, twirling facts.

The Facttracker has been the Facttracker for fifty years the Facttracker is exactly five feet eight inches tall the Facttracker's favorite food is artichokes the Facttracker has one brother and no sisters the Facttracker invented the Funky Facttracker the Facttracker looks good in blue and red but not yellow the Facttracker has an innie belly button the Facttracker once swallowed a giant fib the Facttracker is left-handed the Facttracker has a birthmark on his right shoulder that is reminiscent of El Greco's painting of Toledo with a hint of Diego Rodríguez de Silva y Velázquez's masterwork Las Meninas *the Fact-tracker has a dozen tuna fish sandwiches stuffed in his pockets the Facttracker . . .*

"Do you see anything?" asked the Facttracker.

"It's . . . amazing," whispered the just small enough boy in absolute wonder.

"I'm impressed," said the Facttracker. "It took me weeks to see my first fact. You would have made an excellent facttracker." He then added: "A career that is sadly no longer an option for anyone."

The just small enough boy carefully placed the veriscope in his pants pocket and rubbed his eyes. "I never knew facttracking was so hard on the eyes," he said, blinking.

"It's far harder on the brain," said the Facttracker.

The just small enough boy looked at the floor thoughtfully. "Would—wouldn't this veriscope have worked on me?" he asked. "Couldn't you have just told me my new facts at any time?"

"I'm afraid not," said the Facttracker, shaking his head. "Believe me, I wish it were that simple. But your facts were lost. And I need to track the lost ones before I can track any new ones. Facts build off facts. You need to know that there's an earth before you can know that it's round. You need to know it's round before you can find out how round. Until your initial facts are recovered, all your new ones will stay with them."

The Facttracker noticed how sad this was making the just small enough boy and quickly shifted his mood.

"Cheer up," said the Facttracker warmly. "We're moments away from finding your old and your new facts."

The just small enough boy looked up and smiled.

"I'll bet you must be quite tired of being the just small enough boy," said the Facttracker.

"It's probably the worst name of all time," mumbled the just small enough boy, shuffling his feet embarrassedly.

"Well, I'll certainly agree that it's a terrible name, but it's not the worst name of all time."

"It's not?"

"No," said the Facttracker. "The worst name of all time is Stinky."

"Wow. You must know a fact about everything!"

"Oh, I do," answered the Facttracker. "But that wasn't a fact. It was just my opinion."

The just small enough boy laughed, and the Facttracker made his way over to the far end of the room.

"Well, I suppose this is as good a time as any to turn the Factory on," said the Facttracker. "Now we'll see just how far our knowledge will go. I would have done it earlier, but it's been a bit of a busy day for me, what with all the dancing and all."

He turned around and began pressing a variety of buttons and pulling a host of levers and occasionally spinning a knob here and there.

A warm, unfamiliar feeling filled the just small enough boy, and for perhaps the first time in his life he smiled a just large enough smile. It actually hurt his cheeks, but in a good way.

"Now please, make yourself at home, relax," said the Facttracker. "In just a few moments your search will be over. And then we can both throw up our hats in celebration: to the end of long quests! Of course, I don't actually have a hat, and yours is really more of a cap, so we'll just have to throw up our *metaphorical* hats."

The just small enough boy remembered what the townspeople said about taking off his hat. So he took it off and hung it up on what looked like a hat hook but was actually a big metal lever. As he did, the Facttracker shouted one word: no. But it sounded like this: **NOOOOOOOOO!!!!** The just small enough boy did not know why.

This is why.

CHAPTER 8

Why?

!
☺

OW, THE JUST SMALL enough boy knew a lot
for his age. Unlike most of the townspeople
of Traäkerfaxx, he actually paid attention
to the facts that he found and sold. In fact, for a
boy of his size, he had an awful lot of facts
crammed into his head. But there were still many,
many facts that he didn't have, several in particular that would have served him well at that
moment. They were these:

⊚ That years before, when he was building
the Factory, the Facttracker had included
in his design a Self-Destruct Button.

⚡ That, before completing the Factory, he decided that a Self-Destruct Button was a bad idea because someone might accidentally press it.

 And that potatoes were in fact still outselling sweet potatoes even though most people secretly preferred sweet potatoes over potatoes.

Ah, but surely, you must surely be saying, "So what? None of those facts is important!" And you'd *almost* be right. That's because there's one more fact that he didn't know. And it was this:

😊 That the Facttracker later changed the Self-Destruct Button to a Self-Destruct Lever.

CHAPTER 9

The Explosion

YOU MUST AGREE THAT this last fact was important or, if not important, then at least not wholly unimportant. But important or not, the just small enough boy didn't know it. And so when he took his hat off and politely put it down on the silver lever on the instrument panel, it had an immediate and cataclysmic effect.

When the townspeople heard the explosion, they were taken completely by surprise. They didn't know about the hat or the lever or the potatoes. All they knew was that the just small enough boy had gone into the Factory and several hours later the Factory exploded. They decided right there and then that they wouldn't send any more just small enough boys into the Factory.

But before they had time to make any more decisions, something even more dramatic happened. A large hunk of metal—the roof of the Factory, to be precise—landed with a resounding thud a foot away from the mayor.

"Falling things!" yelled the mayor, dropping his bullfrog and running off as fast as his stubby legs would carry him, which, frankly, wasn't all that fast. It certainly wasn't fast enough to avoid what came next: the boiling plastic. A scalding drop hit him in the seat of his pants, and he let out a high-pitched squeal.

Dodging first the hail of metal, then the rainstorm of plastic, the townspeople scattered in every direction. Above them a frenetic neon cloud was forming in the night sky. The townspeople had never seen anything like it. Then they saw something else they'd never seen before, the Facttracker and the just small enough boy running out from the ruins of the Factory as a fireball exploded behind them and tens of thousands of hundreds of millions of facts shot into the sky.

Everywhere you looked there were facts: Hairy dogs have more hair than hairless dogs: there is

no letter W in the name Rutherford; *rhyme and lime rhyme*. But worst of all, hovering curiously above them, was the fact that potatoes sell better than sweet potatoes.

"I knew it!" shouted the other man in the other scarf.

It seemed like a long time but was really only

a few moments before the Facttracker and the just small enough boy made it safely back to where the townspeople were. But of course *safely* is a very subjective word. The just small enough boy had a look on his face that implied he felt anything but safe. He was white as a powdered albino ghost and shivering terribly. Right after he had triggered the Self-Destruct Lever, the Facttracker had grabbed him and leaped with startling speed onto the banister. Now, I know what you're thinking: Sliding down a half mile of spiral banister must be tremendously fun! True. But sliding down a half mile of spiral banister while an enormous fact-filled fireball chases you down is not.

The townspeople immediately began asking questions.

"Why did the Factory explode?"

"Where are all our facts?"

"Are potatoes more popular than *yams*?"

The just small enough boy tried to speak but found that he couldn't. He looked up at the Facttracker for help. The Facttracker took a deep breath and prepared to speak. But when he finally opened his mouth, it was not words at all that came out but a terrible, horrible wail. The Facttracker was crying.

After a few moments the Facttracker stopped crying and the just small enough boy was able to speak. In fact, they both said the exact same thing at the exact same time.

"I was so close."

CHAPTER 10

*A Tiny Chapter That Isn't Really a Chapter at All
So Much as a Really Long Chapter Title
Placed Strategically to Waste a Bit of Time
in Order to Give the Facttracker
and the Just Small Enough Boy
a Moment to Compose Themselves*

CHAPTER 11

I Don't Know If That Was Enough Time,
but We Have to Get On with the Story

"WHERE ARE OUR facts, Facttracker?" the mayor cried in a panicked voice.

"Fellow Traäkerfaxxians!" shouted the Facttracker suddenly, quieting everyone into instant and absolute silence. "We must remain calm. Things, many of them bad, have happened here. Much is disrupted, but all is *not* lost."

"Well, exactly how much lost are we talking about here?" huffed the mayor. "I can't gauge how outraged and terrified I should be until I know exactly how much is lost."

"There is no reason to be outraged and terrified at all," said the Facttracker. "What we need now is calm." The Facttracker bent down and looked at the just small enough boy with complete seriousness. "Do you still have the veriscope?" he asked.

The just small enough boy nodded silently and reached into his pocket. But the instant his fingers touched the veriscope, he knew something bad had happened. The slide down the banister had wreaked havoc on the contents of his pocket, worst of all on the veriscope. It was in several pieces, and all but one of its "branches" had snapped off.

"I don't think it survived the trip down," said the just small enough boy in a tiny, shaky voice.

The Facttracker sighed and turned to the mayor, who was already red in the face and beginning to swell with frustration.

"The veriscope is damaged," explained the Facttracker calmly. "So the most important thing right now is to find the seed of truth."

"What's a seed of truth?" asked the mayor.

"It's the thing at the heart of all facts, and it was the foundation of the Factory. I could never have built the Factory without it. I can assemble another veriscope if I have to, but the seed is precious. We have to search for it immediately."

"We?" interrupted the mayor. "Why should *we* go looking for facts? *We* are not the Facttracker. *You* are the Facttracker. If anyone should go looking for facts, it should be you, the Facttracker."

"But—"

"So go get our facts for us, Facttracker, and be quick about it," said the mayor with an air of finality.

"I'll help you," said the just small enough boy timidly. He didn't know what else to say and felt certain that the Facttracker would tell him to go away. But the Facttracker didn't say a word. Instead he quietly looked down at the just small enough boy and smiled sadly. And without a word they headed off together into the wreckage, as the townspeople watched from the side.

"What does it look like?" asked the just small enough boy.

"Trust me," said the Facttracker. "You'll know it when you see it."

At first it was exciting. The night was cool, but the heat from the smoldering Factory provided some nice warmth. And even though there were no lights, the huge pieces of metal that littered the ground gave off a bright orange glow that lit their way through the maze of debris.

But as the minutes slipped by and they still hadn't found what the Facttracker was looking for, it became more and more depressing. And very quickly the Facttracker, who had started off confident and sure, became anxious and confused.

"It's *got* to be here!" the Facttracker shouted. "Where else could it have gone? It doesn't make sense!"

Upon hearing this, the mayor picked up his bullfrog and stomped menacingly over to the Facttracker.

"So where are our facts, Facttracker?" he barked.

The Facttracker brushed himself off and tried to explain the situation calmly.

"Okay, everyone, I'm not going to lie to you—"

"He hasn't found them yet!" shouted the mayor.

"Get us our facts back, Facttracker!" shouted someone in the crowd, which quickly surrounded them.

"We have thousands of orders that we need to fill today!" shouted someone else. "Orders for facts!"

The Facttracker stood his ground and made one last plea. "Look, believe me, I understand how important this is to your economy," he begged. "But there are more important things at stake here. Facts aren't just a commodity. They're the cornerstone of civilization! They're as important as the air we breathe! They're—"

And that's when the potato hit him square in the face.

The just small enough boy watched in horror as the dazed Facttracker wiped the potato slop from his eyes only to be hit with another one. Then another. And then another.

"Stop it!" the just small enough boy cried. "He's trying his best! What good is hitting him with potatoes going to do?"

But the tuber barrage continued until the townspeople were finally out of potatoes.

And then someone threw a yam. It caught the Facttracker squarely on the nose, and the result was instantaneous. The Facttracker mumbled something that sounded like EEP and then crumpled to the ground, completely out cold.

It was a dark moment for Traäkerfaxx, which was ironic since the sun was just beginning to rise over the ruins of the Factory.

It seemed as though all was lost.

Until a voice—a sharp, bright, mesmerizing

voice—leaped out from the back of the crowd. This is what it said: "What a magnificent opportunity!"

Every face, even the just small enough boy's, turned to see who had said it.

CHAPTER 12

Who Said It, and Why

T HE CROWD PARTED down the middle, revealing a rather lanky man in a perfectly fitting, although somewhat out-of-date, white suit, smiling a large mouthful of blindingly white teeth and holding a business card in his outstretched hand.

"Pleased to meet you," he said, and flipped the card out of his hand with a snap of his long fingers. The card evaporated in a cloud of silvery smoke, leaving behind a sparkling, scintillating trail of dust. As it hovered in the air, the dust formed into glittering, undulating words:

PROFESSOR L. I. ERSATZ
DOER, SELLER, BUYER, AND TELLER
OF THIS AND THAT

The crowd gasped, then ooohed, then aaahed, and finally erupted in impressed applause. The man flashed his chalky teeth again, and a glint of self-satisfaction flickered in his eyes. The mayor stepped forward.

"My goodness!" The mayor chuckled. "We all are certainly impressed. That was mightily impressive! You are an impressive individual! But who *are* you?"

"I have many names," said the man, flashing his smile at the townspeople like a spotlight. "Some people call me the Fauxtracker; others simply call me a miracle. My name is Ersatz, but you can call me whatever you wish."

He then did a quick little jig and snapped his sinewy fingers, which sent a lightninglike green flash across the sky.

"My oh my! You are by far the most impressive thing I have ever seen!" exclaimed the mayor as he and everyone in the town erupted in even louder applause than before.

"Yes, I am. And it's a good thing too," said the man, smiling even wider than before, "since I am here to save your town."

A collective gasp went out through the crowd.

"Did you hear that?" said the mayor with a sigh

of relief. "We're saved! And just in time too. How lucky is that, Facttracker!"

But the Facttracker was still unconscious.

The mayor, on the other hand, let out a loud squeak of delight. "Well, that's wonderful!" he exclaimed with uncontrolled excitement. "Just wonderful! You are a wonderful individual!"

"Thank you," said Ersatz, smiling more broadly than either of the previous times he had smiled.

"Mayor . . . ," the just small enough boy interjected, but no one was listening to him.

"Please, Mr. Ersatz," pleaded the mayor, "tell us how you plan to save us. Tell us how you'll get our facts back."

Ersatz guffawed. "Facts," he said defiantly, "are for chumps. Are you a chump?"

"Goodness, no," said the mayor.

"Well, that's a relief," said Ersatz, "because I couldn't help people who were chumps. No, Mr. Mayor, I plan on rebuilding your entire town. I plan to make Traäkerfaxx the most successful town in the world. And facts have no part of it! Aren't you tired of dealing with facts anyway?"

"Oh, goodness, yes!" agreed the mayor.

"Wouldn't you rather have a brand-new industry? One that needs no facts at all?"

"Oh yes, yes indeed!"

"Well, I can give it to you," exclaimed Ersatz, his eyes narrowing with intensity. "And when I am done, your economy will be a thousand times more massive than before!"

"A thousand?" squealed the mayor.

"Let's make it a million!"

"Gracious!" shouted the mayor uncontrollably. "But how? How will you do this?"

"We will produce . . . ," began Ersatz, and then paused for dramatic effect.

"Yeeees," prodded the mayor.

"We will produce, process, and sell . . ."

"Oh please, oh please, what?" begged the mayor, hopping up and down with excitement.

"Lies!" exclaimed Ersatz.

A gasp of shock erupted from the crowd.

"Lies?" The mayor gulped. "But aren't lies . . . bad? Aren't they hideous and socially unacceptable things to be avoided by decent folk at all costs?"

"Oh, no, Mr. Mayor," said Ersatz, shaking his head with pity. "Lies are just facts with more personality."

"Really?" said the mayor.

"Oh, yes," continued Ersatz, "and they're far

less work too. No more worrying about getting it right anymore. The only time a lie is wrong is when it's right. A lie can be anything."

"Anything?" said the mayor, excited again.

"Anything!"

"Well, how do they work?" asked the mayor.

"Ah. Quite simply."

"And—and people like them?" asked the mayor.

"They love them!" said Ersatz. "If you'll allow me, I'll demonstrate."

Ersatz stepped forward, smiled, cleared his throat, and then smiled once more. He paused dramatically, and then finally, just when the townspeople could wait no more, he spoke. "You are all geniuses!" he announced.

The townspeople exploded in applause.

"He's so right!" said a man in a blue vest.

"I always suspected I was a genius, but no one ever told me before," said a woman with an umbrella.

"What's a genius?" asked a man with thinning hair.

Ersatz cleared his throat again, and the crowd went completely silent.

"You are also beautiful, talented, interesting,

and clever!" he announced.

"My goodness!" exclaimed the mayor. "Is that true?"

"Do you like hearing it?" asked Ersatz

"Why, I love hearing it!" said the mayor, bursting with pride.

"Then it's true *enough*," replied Ersatz. "And people love things that they love to hear. As I look around right now, do you know what I see? I see happy faces in a happy crowd in a happy town. And do you know why they're happy? Because of what I said. That's right. Was it true? Who knows? But it made you happy. I am in the happiness business. And I'm here to offer you a part of that. Before I go on, I'd like to ask you one question, and I want you to think about it. What have facts ever done for you?"

"Nothing!" shouted the mayor enthusiastically.

"That's right," said Ersatz after a few moments. "Nothing but imprisonment."

A thoughtful *ooh* went through the crowd.

"You have been imprisoned by these facts. They are nothing but a jail. If I tell you that the world is round and that that's a fact, well, what can you do about it? That's it. It's round. How boring! But what if I told you that the world could be flat? Or square! Or an eighteen-sided polygon! How much more exciting is that?"

"So much!" shouted the mayor with glee.

"That's right!" exclaimed Ersatz. "Because I'm not just in the lie business; I'm also in the excitement business. And a lie is almost always more interesting than the truth. Mr. Mayor, would you be kind enough to tell me what you did yesterday?"

"Me?" said the mayor, pleased and proud that someone was interested in his day. "Oh, well, let's see. I woke up. Yes, I woke up, and then I ate some breakfast. It was oatmeal, I believe. Then I stared into space for a while. After that it was time for lunch. I had a ham sandwich, with a side of Tater Tots. Then I bit my toenails for a while and went to bed."

There was a long, long silence as everyone absorbed the dreariness of the mayor's day. Finally Ersatz spoke. "That's lovely," he said. "But now let me tell you what you did yesterday . . . using lies. First you were awoken by your butler, Reginald, who greeted you with your customary eggs Benedict and the morning paper. Whilst reading the paper, you noticed an article describing how the ozone layer is vanishing. Outraged, you immediately descended into your cavernous underground laboratory, where you invented a machine that would restore the ozone layer *and* make butterscotch ice cream at the same time. Having saved the earth from certain doom, you then sat down to a splendid lunch of Beluga caviar and pâté. But not before saving the world *four more times*! Once with a meteor detector, once with giant mutant mosquito repellent, and twice by reversing time and setting things right again. Then you trimmed your award-winning toenails and were tucked into bed by God himself."

The crowd enthusiastically cheered the mayor.

"My word!" exclaimed the mayor with delight. "I never noticed how exciting I am!"

"When you use lies, *everyone* is exciting!" said Ersatz.

"I want to be exciting," shouted a woman who once ate two and a half ants on a dare.

"Yes, I too would like to be exciting. So exciting it makes people say, 'Hey, look at that exciting guy over there. Man, is he exciting!'" said an unmemorable man.

"We need lies!" yelled a woman in back. "Give us lies!"

"Yeah," said a man in the front, "we can't live without lics!"

"People of Traäkerfaxx," Ersatz announced majestically, "I shall give you all the lies you will ever need! No more waking up early. No more lining up at the Factory. No more waiting for the Facttracker to send you his hand-me-downs. From now on all you have to do is ask. And you don't even have to do that if you're not in the mood!"

The crowd was so thunderously overjoyed that not a single person heard the pained groans of the man waking up on the ground behind them. That man of course was the Facttracker.

~~CHAPTER 13~~

There Will Not Be a Chapter 13 Because It Might Be Unlucky and the Facttracker Needs All the Luck He Can Get Now

CHAPTER 14

Unfortunately for the Facttracker, Even Mentioning Chapter 13 Turned Out to Be Enough to Bring Him Bad Luck. Although It Might Just Be That This Wasn't a Lucky Day for Him to Begin With

THE JUST SMALL ENOUGH boy sighed with relief when he finally heard the Facttracker's groans. During Ersatz's speech he had remained at the Facttracker's side, trying everything he could think of to wake him. When nothing worked, he decided the least he could do was pick the yam bits out of his beard. But even that proved fruitless since the bits seemed to find their way into the deepest recesses of the beard, and the just small enough boy quickly grew squeamish. Judge if you must, but if you've ever had to pick yam bits out of an old man's bushy beard, I'm sure you'd forgive him.

The just small enough boy helped the Facttracker to his feet.

"What happened?" asked the Facttracker, rubbing his head.

"The townspeople hit you with a bunch of potatoes," answered the just small enough boy. "And then a yam."

The Facttracker steadied himself and looked around at the crowd of townspeople nearby. "What are they doing?" he asked. "Did they find the seed?"

"Oh, no," said the just small enough boy. "They're listening to the stranger from out of town. He says he can help us. He's a professor too."

"Really?" said the Facttracker. "I wonder who he is."

"His name's Ersatz."

The Facttracker's eyes went wide. He spun toward the mayor with such urgent speed that his beard whipped around, flinging out every last bit of yam onto the just small enough boy.

"Mayor! I must speak with you!" shouted the Facttracker as he ran through the crowd.

"What *is* it, Facttracker!" demanded the mayor. "*What* is *so* important that you're interrupting

78

this fine, impressive gentleman?"

"I must speak to you in private immediately," said the Facttracker, deliberately ignoring Ersatz. "And this man is *neither* fine *nor* impressive."

"Oh, really. And why is that?"

"Because he is not to be trusted."

"Well, how do you know that?"

"I know it," answered the Facttracker, "because he is my brother."

A new gasp, even gaspier than all the previous gasps, ran amok through the crowd.

"Is this true, Mr. Ersatz?" asked the mayor. "Is it true that you're his brother?"

Ersatz turned to the Facttracker, smiled slyly, and then looked the mayor directly in the eyes. "No," he said, "it is not true at all."

"Well then," said the mayor jovially, "that settles it. The word of Mr. Ersatz is good enough for me. If he says he's not someone's brother, then he's not someone's brother."

"But just look at him!" protested the Facttracker. "He looks just like me!"

It was true. Ersatz did look almost identical to the Facttracker. He seemed a bit younger and had a pencil-thin black mustache where the Facttracker sported a beard, and he seemed a bit more spry and cunning, and his eyes shifted a bit more than the Facttracker's, and he was wearing a white suit instead of the constellation-print Facttracker uniform, but otherwise he looked exactly like the Facttracker.

"No, I don't," said Ersatz flatly.

"Yes, you do!" shouted the Facttracker.

"I have a mustache, you have a beard," said Ersatz.

"Your face," said the Facttracker, "your face looks just like mine."

"No, it doesn't."

"It does!" said the Facttracker. "Okay, we're exactly the same height. We are *precisely* the same height."

"No, we're not."

"We are! Surely you can't deny that!"

"I just did," said Ersatz innocently.

The Facttracker pleaded with the townspeople. "You *cannot* trust this man," he said. "He is a liar."

"No, I'm not," said Ersatz.

"He's lying right now!" said the Facttracker.

The mayor stepped forward, inserting himself in between the two mostly identical men.

"Now, I'm not one to say who is or isn't identical," he said with an inflated air of dignified sagacity. "If Mr. Ersatz wants to look dissimilar from someone, well, then that's his business, I should imagine. Is it for me to tell him to look like someone else? I think not! A man should look or not look like whomever he pleases. And if Mr. Ersatz *is* lying, as you claim, then shouldn't we listen to those lies and decide whether we like them? Maybe his lies aren't so bad. He seems to think that we can sell them. And if we can sell them, then how bad can they be?"

The townspeople all nodded in complete agreement.

"We need to sell *something*!" exclaimed a man in galoshes.

"And we don't have any facts anymore," said a woman in a purple polka-dotted dress.

"I agree with the mayor *and* I agree with both of the people who agreed with him before me," said an agreeable man in an agreeable sweater.

The mayor smiled broadly and put his arm around Ersatz's shoulder. "Well, it seems that we are all in complete agreement then," he exclaimed jovially.

The Facttracker tried to interrupt, but before he even finished the word *but*, he was roughly shoved aside by the crowd, each and every person in it trying to move closer to Ersatz to tell him how impressive he was.

And in the middle of it all, Ersatz said only one word: "Magnificent!"

CHAPTER 15

A Particularly Long Chapter, but an Important One Nonetheless, So Don't Skip It

OVER THE LAST SEVERAL hours a host of unfortunate developments had befallen the Facttracker. His Factory had exploded, he'd lost all his facts, and he'd been knocked unconscious by a torrent of potatoes and a yam. But by far the most unfortunate of all the unfortunate developments had to be the return of his brother.

And yes, Ersatz was the Facttracker's brother. In fact, he was his *twin* brother.

But surely, you must surely be asking, if Ersatz was the Facttracker's twin brother, then how come no one had ever heard of him? Good question. And the answer is this: Ersatz wasn't just the

Facttracker's twin brother; he was the Facttracker's *long-lost* twin brother.

Actually, Ersatz wasn't really lost so much as banished. He was the Facttracker's long-banished twin brother. He had been banished by the Facttracker's father, who also happened to be Ersatz's father. Why had he been banished? For lying.

Now, there are very few rules that a facttracker must follow. It may be a terribly difficult job, but it is certainly not a terribly regulated job. There is generally only one facttracker, and so there is generally no one looking over the facttracker's shoulder to make sure he is doing everything correctly. Unless, that is, he is a facttracker in training.

And long ago, when they were still as small as the just small enough boy, both Ersatz and his brother were facttrackers *in training*. They were training under their father. It was their father's idea that the job, which had taken up most of his time and all of his life, would be far more manageable if split between two rather than piled high atop one.

He worked his sons day and night, hour after hour, drilling them and teaching them the ins and outs of facttracking. He taught them how to spot a fact and how to use a veriscope. The two sons worked hard tracking facts, and yet at the end of the day only one son was exhausted. That son was never Ersatz.

No matter how many facts he hauled in, Ersatz seemed as spry and energetic as he was when the day began. This was particularly amazing since he hauled in thousands and thousands of facts. His brother, on the other hand, brought in only a few dozen. To be honest, a few dozen was pretty good, especially for a facttracker in training. But Ersatz broke all previous records and certainly any expectations. And the more facts he hauled in, the more praise he received from his father.

"My goodness!" his father would exclaim at the end of the day. "This is most impressive! Most impressive indeed! You are an impressive individual, Ersatz!" And he would proudly put his arm around young Ersatz's shoulder and sing his praises all through the rest of the night. Their father didn't mean to ignore his other son—in fact, he loved him dearly—but he was so overwhelmed and impressed with Ersatz that he couldn't help himself.

And who could blame him? There wasn't a person who met Ersatz who didn't take an instant liking to him. He was outgoing, intelligent, friendly, courteous, and full of fun little tricks. But the thing that most people noticed immediately—the thing that you couldn't *help* noticing immediately—was his smile. It was bright, warm, disarming, and the purest shade of white that nature had ever produced. Somehow, when you saw it, you just felt that you could trust it.

And everyone *did* trust the smile and the little boy behind it.

But young Ersatz was far from trustworthy. For you see, the enormous loads of facts that he hauled in each and every day contained, in actuality, very few facts at all. In fact, they contained *no* facts. What they did contain was this: untruths. Thousands and thousands of untruths.

Ah, but surely you must be saying, "His father was a facttracker, and surely a facttracker would spot an untruth as quickly as he would spot a fact. There's no way that a facttracker would fall for such a pitiful ruse!" Okay, okay, calm down. The answer to that is a bit complex.

Now, Ersatz may have been an awful facttracker, but he was an absolutely brilliant liar. The lies that he brought home were of the highest quality. And a good lie can be very convincing, even to a facttracker. If you don't take the time to examine information carefully—where it comes from and why it exists—well, most of the time you'll never know the difference. Sometimes fact*checking* is more important than facttracking.

But there's also one other factor that was even more important: The Facttracker loved his son very dearly. The thought, the mere *suggestion* that his son was bringing home untruths instead of facts would have broken his heart. And for a long time he tried to pretend that it wasn't happening.

It was simply one fact that he chose not to track.

Ah, but what about his brother? What about the boy who eventually became the Facttracker? Didn't he say anything?

Well, at first he was merely curious how his brother was so much more prolific than he was. Then, as the days went on, the young Facttracker's curiosity grew into outright suspicion. He tried to tell his father on numerous occasions, but it was a tremendously difficult conversation to have—especially without proof.

But one day, as he was walking through the house, he suddenly heard a strange sound, as though a hundred people were whispering to one another.

Following the voices, he soon found himself at

the door to Ersatz's closet. At the top of the closet, behind a half dozen dusty boxes, was a large black velvet sack. This was strange enough, but what made it even stranger was that it appeared the contents were moving.

Standing on his tiptoes, he managed to move the boxes aside. On the side of the sack, in intricately embroidered gold letters, were the words *My Favorites*.

But just as he was about to open the sack, he suddenly heard the front door open. In a moment of panic he lost his balance and grabbed on to the sack to steady himself.

That's when it happened.

The sack fell down, dumping its contents right on top of the dazed young Facttracker's head.

And what were the contents? Hundreds upon hundreds of lies. These were not just little white lies either. No, they were **big**, **dirty**, barefaced, whopping lies. Even worse, there were lies of every kind: *rumors*, *fibs*, **unfounded accusations**, guesstimates, *slanders*, libels, hyperboles, *perjuries*, calumnies, exaggerations, and tall tales.

It was a horrible sight for anyone, but it was especially horrible for a young Facttracker who had his head buried in an avalanche of them. In a

moment of desperate panic he gasped. And before he knew what had happened, he accidentally swallowed a particularly preposterous fib.

His father came running in when he heard his son coughing fitfully. "Are you all right?" he cried, patting him on the back. "What happened?"

The young Facttracker opened his mouth to explain, but the words that came out were not the words in his head. They were entirely different words that said entirely different things, and he had no control over them.

"Of course I'm okay, Father. I was simply standing here when a large bird swooped down out of nowhere with a giant linguine noodle in its mouth. I thought, *That's odd, a bird with linguine; I should investigate this,* and I went chasing after it, but no sooner had I begun my chase when suddenly I was attacked by a hundred flying saucers! Honest to goodness, genuine flying saucers! 'Well,' I said to myself, 'this certainly is an unusual predicament. Me, a giant bird, a huge pasta noodle, and two hundred flying saucers piloted by talking dogs.' Did I mention that they were piloted by talking dogs? Because that's important. Yeah, they spoke Spanish, which was weird because they were clearly French bulldogs. . . ."

On and on he went, unable to stop himself as the lie grew longer and more complex. His father knew immediately what had happened. He waited patiently for the lie to end and then silently, sadly, carried his exhausted son to his bedroom and gently tucked him in. After he was sure he was asleep, he searched Ersatz's room for the rest of the lies and, with a shudder of disgust, destroyed them.

When Ersatz came home that night, his father was waiting for him. He sat Ersatz down and looked him straight in the eye.

"Son," he said, "now just tell me, and I promise not to get angry, just please tell me: Did you have a sack of lies in your closet?"

Ersatz looked his father straight in the eye. "Nope," he said flatly.

"No, seriously, son," he said, putting a firm but gentle hand on his son's shoulder, "I promise, I won't be angry. I just need to hear the truth."

"Those weren't my lies."

"But I found the sack in your room."

"Someone asked me to hold it for them."

"Who?"

"Gypsies."

"Gypsies? There aren't any Gypsies in Traäkerfaxx."

"Of course there aren't. They were here with the pirate ship."

"The pirate— How did a pirate ship get this far inland?"

"Oh, it was tied to the elephant caravan."

"Why on earth was there an elephant caravan?"

"To carry the swamis, I imagine."

"Swamis? What were swamis doing here?"

"They were in town for the snail watchers' convention."

"There was no snail watchers' convention in Traäkerfaxx!"

"I know. They lost the address, so they were just going from town to town, asking if anyone knew where it was."

"So let me get this straight. You got these lies from elephant-pulled Gypsy pirates, hopping all around the country with swamis looking for a snail watchers' convention? Is that what you're trying to tell me!?"

"Yup."

There was a long pause. "Um, can I meet them?" asked his father, genuinely curious.

"Sorry. They left this morning."

His father had no choice. No matter how much he wanted to deny it, Ersatz was a liar. And although there are very few rules that a fact-tracker must follow, there is one golden rule that cannot, under any circumstance, be broken.

A facttracker must respect the truth.

With no other alternative, he took a deep breath and had the conversation he'd been secretly dreading for years

"Ersatz," he said, "when you and your brother were born, it was the greatest joy in my life. You see, no facttracker had ever had twins before.

Since the dawn of man, give or take a few years, there had always been one facttracker, and he had always had one son. When I had two sons, I naturally assumed that this aberration was the universe's way of alleviating the burden. That you were here to help each other out. But I was wrong. You're *not* here to help each other out. You're here to *balance* each other out. I understand that now. But I don't blame *you*. It's my fault. I had forgotten the laws of nature. 'There can be no such thing as a fact without the existence of lies to distort them. And no such thing as a lie without facts to disprove them.' Do you understand? And while I'll always love you, I'm afraid I can't allow you to become a facttracker." It was the hardest thing he had ever had to say.

Ersatz, however, didn't offer up any objections.

"I understand completely, Father," he reassured him, smiling contritely. "And were I in your shoes, faced with the same unfortunate dilemma, I would no doubt do the same thing. Well, if you'll excuse me, I'll be off to bed. It's been a trying day for all of us, and I should like to reflect upon my misdeeds until such time as sleep overtakes me. I only hope the Good Lord sees fit to provide me with appropriately penitent dreams."

He did not, however, go to sleep. Instead, while everyone else was sleeping, young Ersatz tiptoed into his father's room and took the veriscope. He spent the next several hours pointing it all around the town, collecting information about the past, present, and possible future of Traäkerfaxx. When he was satisfied that he knew everything he could possibly know about the town, he pointed the veriscope at himself.

Smiling wickedly, he snatched a single tiny fact that he kept with him for the next half century. It was this:

Ersatz can remake Traäkerfaxx in his image.

And as he crossed the town line, leaving Traäkerfaxx in the darkness behind him, he muttered one last word: "Magnificent."

Ah, but surely you must be saying, "Chapter 15 is an important chapter! Chapter 15 is a really, *really* important chapter! Why wasn't any of this mentioned earlier?" The answer is simple: I couldn't write chapter 15 until I'd finished the first fourteen chapters.

CHAPTER 16

The Seed of Truth and a Not So True Story About It

BUT ALL THAT WAS in the past. And while it may have explained the Facttracker's predicament in the present, it didn't help him one bit. For in just the short time that it took to read the last chapter, the entire town had fallen completely in love with Ersatz. The townspeople formed a large circle around him, a circle that not only kept Ersatz in but also kept the Facttracker and the just small enough boy out.

"I hereby declare today to be **ERSATZ DAY!**" the mayor declared as he led Ersatz up to a makeshift podium on the half-buried roof of the old Factory. Ersatz beamed from ear to ear, and the more he beamed, the more the crowd cheered.

But they instantly quieted when Ersatz reached into his jacket pocket and pulled out a small, round gray object. Even though it was no bigger than a marble, it gave off so much light that the townspeople had to squint to look at it.

"What's that?" asked the mayor, his eyes practically shut tight with excitement.

"This," said Ersatz, stroking the incandescent orb, "this is a seed."

"A seed? What kind of seed is it?" asked the mayor. "It doesn't look like any I've ever come across. Is it a sweet potato seed?"

"No," said Ersatz. "This is a seed of truth. And it is at the heart of all lies."

"Really?" asked the mayor. "The Facttracker said it was at the heart of all facts."

"It's at the heart of all lies too," explained Ersatz.

The mayor raised his eyebrows and snorted. "Well, it doesn't look so special to me, if you ask me," he said.

"Perhaps not," conceded Ersatz. "But looks are but a small part of anything. Who would imagine that the tiny monarch butterfly contains enough venom to kill twenty great apes?"

"It does?" asked the mayor, impressed.

"If you like the sound of it, then it absolutely does," said Ersatz.

"My goodness, the monarch is an impressive butterfly!" exclaimed the mayor.

"And this is an impressive seed," said Ersatz.

"My oh my," said the mayor. "Where did you find such an impressive seed?"

"Ah," said Ersatz, "how I came across this seed is a great story, a great story indeed. It was in my youth, during one of my many exploits across the far exotic, mysterious lands of the world. I had passed unharmed through the Curious Caverns of Mirrored Splendorosity, narrowly escaped the Indescribably Dynamic Desert of Exploding Dandelions, and nearly perished in the Figuratively Electrifying Mountain Hall of the Inconceivably Bizarre Mountain Hall King. But it had all been worth it. For there, in front of me, in its unbelievable gloriosity, stood the final goal in my quest, the much fabled, never discovered, and thoroughly unclassifiable seed of truth."

The crowd, which had been collectively holding its breath, exhaled.

"Yes," continued Ersatz, "but even as I looked upon the seed, I knew my adventure was far from over. Danger lay both behind *and* before me! For I still had to pass through the Astoundingly Inexplicable Underwater Caves of the Peculiar Popping Mermaids and then make my way past the Stupefying Salami Statues of the Seven Salamander—"

"Thief!" A voice from the back interrupted.

The crowd turned around and saw the Facttracker, red and panting with anger.

"That man is a thief," he shouted, pointing accusingly at Ersatz. "That's my seed! He must have stolen it from the rubble of the Factory!"

"Is this true, Ersatz?" asked the mayor.

"Now, which story sounds more likely?" asked Ersatz. "His, which is dull and boring, or mine, which is full of interesting and specific details?"

"Oh, well, the one with all the interesting details, of course," said the mayor happily.

"He's lying!" screamed the Facttracker.

Ersatz took a deep, deliberate breath. "Now Mr. Mayor," he began, "what I am about to do is a complex and dangerous operation. It requires complete concentration. Even the *slightest* distraction, and I could accidentally ruin the *entire* process. And then where would you be? Without any lies, that's where. Do you see where I'm going with this?"

The mayor smiled happily at him. "Not at all," he said.

"If the Facttracker is going to keep distracting me," said Ersatz, "then I can't do this. And if I can't do this, then I have no reason to be here. Do you follow?"

The mayor smiled even more happily. "Nope," he said.

"Will you please have the Facttracker restrained!" boomed Ersatz.

"Oooh! Oh, of course!" said the mayor.

And within half a moment the Facttracker was rudely grabbed by several townspeople, one of whom placed a not too clean hand over the Facttracker's mouth, silencing him.

The just small enough boy wanted desperately to help. But unlike the Facttracker, he had not managed to push his way past the crowd. And so all he could do was watch helplessly from the outside. Fortunately, he had a just decent enough view.

CHAPTER 17

What the Just Small Enough Boy Saw

FROM HIS OTHER pocket, Ersatz whipped out a small burlap pouch that was tied at the top by a long black thread. The pouch seemed to move—to *pulse*—as though there were a million tiny squirmy things in it. That's because there *were* a million tiny squirmy things in it.

The crowd gathered closer to get a better look. "Ooh, what's in there?" asked the mayor, poking a pudgy finger out to prod the pouch.

"This," said Ersatz, pulling the pouch away, "is the beginning of your new industry. It is a pouch of untruths. Baby untruths, to be precise. They want desperately to become fully grown lies. But they have no direction. No heart. They don't know what to lie about. Not yet."

Ersatz untied the top of the pouch slowly, and one or two tiny untruths peeked out from the top. The untruths looked like teensy-tiny, itsy-bitsy little fortune cookie papers, except that these papers moved around and squeaked. It was hard to make out what they were saying, but it sounded sort of like "really" and "I swear" and "no, honestly."

"Aww. Aren't they cute?" said Ersatz, gently petting them with his thumb. "The untruths are trying to convince us. Now let's give them something to convince us of."

"They talk?" asked the mayor, confused. "How come they talk? Facts don't talk. Facts just have words written on them."

"Oh, lies prefer not to put anything down in writing," explained Ersatz. "It's easier for them to change their story this way."

He stuffed the seed of truth into the pouch and then quickly tied it up again. Immediately a strange suctionlike sound emanated from within the bag. It was the sound of a million tiny squirming untruths latching on to the seed. The pouch throbbed with energy.

"This is going to be the end of your troubles,

Mr. Mayor," said Ersatz as he held the pouch up and examined it happily. "The end of scrounging around for facts, the end of relying on the Facttracker, the end of the old, boring, traditional Traäkerfaxx."

"But what is it now?" asked the mayor, scratching his head not so much in confusion as in itchiness.

"It is," said Ersatz with an air of finality, "a beginning."

CHAPTER 18

The Beginning and What Happened When It Began to Begin

WHAT HAPPENED NEXT was totally and completely unexpected to every single person in Traäkerfaxx—everyone, that is, but Ersatz, who not only expected it but made it happen. Ersatz took the pouch and brought it over to the charred patch of dirt where the Factory had once stood. The townspeople, completely captivated and baffled by what he was doing, followed him silently. He then dug a hole about a foot deep and inspected it. He measured its height and its width and its depth and made several small adjustments that only he seemed to understand. When he was properly satisfied with the hole, he carefully placed the pouch in it and then covered the whole thing up again.

"There," he said, looking up at the bewildered townspeople, "all done." There was a long, awkward pause as everyone in the town, not quite sure what to make of this turn of events, looked at everyone else in the town.

"Well, that was mightily unimpressive!" huffed the mayor. "You dug a hole! *I* could have dug a hole! What do you expect us to do now?"

"Wait," said Ersatz calmly.

The townspeople waited, and waited, and waited, and waited, and waited, and waited, and waited, and waited, and waited, and waited, and then stopped waiting.

"You have to keep waiting," said Ersatz.

So they waited some more. Then a bit more. Then, finally, when they could wait not a fraction of a moment longer, they heard a sound. It was a deep rumbling—a growl, almost—coming from the earth below them.

"Um, Ersatz," said the mayor nervously, "is this what we were waiting for?"

"It is, Mr. Mayor, it is," said Ersatz, smiling wider than ever.

Suddenly the townspeople felt themselves

lifted up as the ground bulged below them in squiggly lines, darting all across and in and out, like a hundred fire hoses filling with water.

"What are they?" squealed the mayor.

"Roots, Mr. Mayor!" proclaimed Ersatz vibrantly. "Great, giant roots!"

The roots snaked their way across the field and continued to burrow beneath the rest of Traäkerfaxx.

"Ersatz, what is the meaning of—," the mayor demanded.

"Watch!" shouted Ersatz, pointing to the center of the chaos.

All eyes looked over just in time to see the earth bubble furiously. And then from the very center of it a pale face popped up.

It was Ersatz.

Well, not *actually* Ersatz. It was a statue of Ersatz, smiling obsequiously and holding up his right hand truthfully. Up, up he went, pushed by some great force below him. And then the towns-people saw what was pushing him: a building! An enormous stone building with giant stone columns jutting down and two huge stone lions guarding the front. The stone was so polished and unnatural that it may as well have been made from a mirror, a rounded and warped mirror. As the structure rose out of the earth, the townspeople watched their own twisted reflections in wordless wonder.

When the rumbling finally stopped and the building settled down atop its immense stone roots, not a person in Traäkerfaxx knew quite how to describe it. *Big* would be a good word to use. *Curious* would also work. "A big, curious, mystifying building that seemed to evoke both hope and dread in all who looked upon it" would also have sufficed. But only if you also mentioned the large gold sign above the lions that read: **OVER 0 LIES SERVED!**

"My goodness," whispered the mayor in hushed reverence, "that is so impressive."

Ersatz stepped forward, a blinding white smile across his face. "People of Traäkerfaxx," he said, "I present you with . . . the Liebrary!"

CHAPTER 19

The Liebrary

THERE WAS NO GASP from the townspeople. There was no sound at all. Everyone was completely silent. Well, maybe not *completely* silent. If you listened very closely, you might catch the sound of an occasional gulp or maybe the feathery flutter of a hundred befuddled eyes blinking in unison. In fact, there is only one word that could accurately describe what the townspeople felt: *awe*.

"I take it by your silence that you approve," said Ersatz happily.

"Goodness, yes, we approve wholeheartedly!" the mayor exhaled. "But what is it?"

"This," said Ersatz with great pride, "this is the future. It is the future of Traäkerfaxx. It is the future of the world. This is the heart of all things to come."

"Ah!" said the mayor, delighted. "That's wonderful, just wonderful!" There was a long pause, and then he asked, "But what *is* it?"

"Why, my dear Mr. Mayor," said Ersatz, putting his arm around the mayor's shoulder, "this beautiful structure you see before you is the one, the *only* . . . Liebrary. It is a means of mass-producing misleading misrepresentations, Mr. Mayor! Yes, sir, this splendorous stone edifice is the mother lode of mischief, malfeasance, and moral mange. And it's all yours!"

A great cheer erupted from the crowd. "Moral mange!" exclaimed the mayor with mindless delight. "I had no idea we were getting moral mange! And the mother lode no less! You are a great, great man, Ersatz, a great, great man indeed!"

Ersatz bared his brilliant teeth and gingerly led the mayor over to a large stone button at the base of the steps.

"This button begins the process, Mr. Mayor. By pressing it, you will be whisking Traäkerfaxx into the future. And not just anywhere in the future, the front of it!"

Everyone in the crowd applauded enthusiastically; even the man with the not too clean hands began to clap.

That was all the Facttracker needed. He shook himself free and, in a last desperate attempt, ran up to the mayor and grabbed him by the scruff of his jacket.

"Mr. Mayor," he pleaded, "you *can't* press that button. It will only bring us ruin!"

"Didn't you just hear what Ersatz said?" retorted the mayor. "We're going to be at the front of the future. That's the best part of the future to be in!"

With that, he pushed the button.

Ersatz smiled wickedly as the Facttracker dropped his head in defeat. Behind them the Liebrary began to shake violently. A powerful grinding sound burst from inside. There was the noise of machines, great unseen machines hard at work, bustling and molding countless unseen somethings.

"What's happening?" shouted the mayor. "What's it doing?"

"It is making your product, Mr. Mayor," said

Ersatz calmly. "Inside, there are exactly two thousand four hundred eighty-seven rooms, all filled with the most complex state-of-the-art machinery imaginable. And all those machines are working their hardest to develop, produce, and process the most complex state-of-the-art lies. And they are doing it all just for you. Wait, any minute now . . ."

And the noise stopped.

There was a long breathless moment as everyone waited to see what would happen next. What happened next was this: The stone lions in front opened their eyes. They blinked twice, yawned great, cavernous, stone yawns, looked around at the townspeople, and then spoke.

"You are all geniuses."

CHAPTER 20

The Lions

WITH THE LIEBRARY'S very first lie, the sign above the lions clicked forward from **0** to **1**. But what the lions said was only the beginning—a very bad beginning—and it quickly got worse.

"Snowmen are made of snow and firemen are made of fire," said the first lion.

"There are three days in a week and seven weeks in a minute," said the second lion.

"George Washington liked to water-ski," said the first lion.

"Queen Elizabeth could burp the alphabet," said the second lion.

As the minutes passed, the Liebrary steadily increased its production and the lions increased the number of lies that they spoke. The counter above the Liebrary clicked continuously.

"Humans didn't evolve; they hatched," said the first lion—*click*—**30**.

"Socks are meant to be smelly," said the second lion—*click*—**44**.

"You should keep your eyes open when you sneeze," said the first lion—*click*—**56**.

"Toe jam tastes great with peanut butter," said the second lion—*click*—**72**.

"Grown-ups know everything," said the first lion—*click*—**91**.

"Lobsters write excellent poetry," said the second lion—*click*—**100**.

The townspeople were thrilled. And no one was more thrilled than the mayor, who placed himself directly beneath the great stone beasts and let the lies cascade down on him like a ticker-tape parade.

"It is so lovely to have an industry again," he giggled. "And one that's so much fun too! When we sold facts, I took no interest in them at all. But now that we have all these lies I can't help taking an interest in them because they're all so interesting.

Especially the ones about me."

"You are a clever, handsome man, Mr. Mayor," said the first lion.

"See?" said the mayor, beaming. "None of the *facts* about me were like that! They all said I was dull, slow witted, and funny looking." And he scowled at the Facttracker, who was sitting on a patch of grass, his head resting dejectedly in his palms.

"Well, Mr. Mayor," said Ersatz, "help yourself to all the lies you want. And when you've sold those, come back for more. There will *always* be lies here for you!"

Smiling proudly, Ersatz left the townspeople to their merriment and walked quietly over to the Facttracker. Without making eye contact or slowing his pace, Ersatz chirped, "C'mon, bro," and walked into the Liebrary's entrance, which was not on the building itself, but in one of the giant roots below it. With a deep groan, the Facttracker stood up slowly and began to follow. Suddenly the just small enough boy ran over and tugged at his sleeve.

"We're going inside? Are you sure that's a good idea?" he said, concerned.

"No, it's probably not," said the Facttracker

sadly. "But *we're* not doing it. You have to stay here."

"But—"

The Facttracker put a firm hand up.

"I'm sorry," he said, and followed Ersatz into the Liebrary.

Of course, as I'm sure you've guessed, the just small enough boy followed him anyway.

CHAPTER 21

*In Which Many Horribly Terrible Things Happen,
So You Shouldn't Read It If You're
Faint of Heart or Simply Don't Like Reading
the Twenty-first Chapter of Books*

THE INSIDE OF THE Liebrary was absolutely magnificent. Enormous stone columns filled the mammoth hall like a petrified forest and stretched up to a ceiling that was breathtaking. Though most of it was cast in shadow, strategically placed spotlights pointed here and there, illuminating points of an elaborate fresco that depicted Ersatz in various acts of kindness and charity. In one story Ersatz could be seen holding a door open for an elderly woman. In another he gave a puppy a sponge bath. Yet another seemed to imply he was Santa Claus.

The just small enough boy tiptoed through the

great room, scurrying through the shadows from column to column as he trailed the Facttracker and Ersatz. Finally the two men reached their destination, and the just small enough boy, afraid to get any closer, hid behind a column.

He watched with bated breath as the Facttracker walked glumly over to where Ersatz was standing. At first the just small enough boy thought Ersatz was between a pair of flickering lightbulbs. But then he realized that they must have been directly behind the two lions out front. Their long stone tails poked out through the wall and wagged back and forth, kicking up bright orange sparks as they scraped the floor.

"It's good to see you again, brother," said Ersatz in a tone that made even the hairs on his *own* arm stand up straight.

The Facttracker stared down at the floor as he spoke in a strained voice. "How could you do this, Ersatz?" he asked.

"How? Quite easily, actually. I've been in Traäkerfaxx for months now. Just watching, taking it all in. You'd be amazed at how many opportunities pop up when all you do is watch. The blueprints you sent the boy told me about the lever; then it was just a matter of getting someone to pull it. I really liked the Factory, by the way. I was sorry to have to make it explode. But you have to do what you have to do, right?"

The Facttracker let out a deep, pained groan.

"I should think you would be happy," Ersatz said. "I am simply continuing your work."

The Facttracker looked up. "That's not true!" he protested. "I tracked facts! You're producing lies!"

"And they are both opposite sides of the same coin," continued Ersatz. "A coin that is far more valuable now."

"More valuable?" choked the Facttracker. "How can you say that?"

"You give people facts about themselves, don't you? Tell them what they are, right? Well, for every thing that we *are*, there are a million things that we're *not*. And usually, those million things are what we really want but can never have. Well, I provide those things."

"Value isn't just measured in money, Ersatz!"

"Money? Do you really think this is about money?" Ersatz laughed. "What do I need money for? I get everything I want with my charming good looks." And he smiled so broadly and brightly that the just small enough boy had to cover his eyes to keep himself from involuntarily starting to like Ersatz. "This isn't about money. It's about the world."

"What you're doing here will destroy the world. It's—it's evil!" shouted the Facttracker.

"Evil?" scoffed Ersatz. "It's no more evil than night is to day, than faith is to science, than fantasy is to reality. You forget your laws of nature too easily, brother. There can be no such thing as a fact without the existence of lies to distort them. And no such thing as a lie without facts to disprove them. Didn't Father teach you anything after I left? We're connected in ways that these people here couldn't possibly understand. You need me. And more important, the world needs me."

The just small enough boy gasped in horror as Ersatz snapped his fingers, and the two lion tails suddenly wrapped around the helpless Facttracker.

"So is this it then?" demanded the Facttracker as he struggled vainly to free himself from the tails. "You're going to kill me?"

Ersatz rolled his eyes. "Did you even hear a *word* of what I've been saying?" He sighed. "Of course I'm not going to kill you. You're my brother. I might *need* you. Laws of nature, remember? But since I can't have you wandering around Traäkerfaxx . . ."

The just small enough boy didn't know what Ersatz was going to do next, but he knew the tone of Ersatz's voice. It was the kind of tone that meant something awful was about to happen. And so he did the only thing he could think of. He reached into his pocket, grabbed a handful of the facts that the Facttracker had given him, crumpled them into a tight little ball, and then hurled the whole thing at Ersatz.

The fact ball struck Ersatz right in the chest, splattering all over his white suit. But far from being annoyed, as the just small enough boy had expected, Ersatz instead spun around and smiled even more broadly and brightly than seemed possible.

"Aah," exclaimed Ersatz happily, "the just small enough boy. If there's *anyone* in this godforsaken town that could benefit from my services, it's him."

"Leave him alone, Ersatz. He's just a child!" shouted the Facttracker, struggling with the stone tails.

"Is that a fact?" said Ersatz wryly. "Well, facts are no longer relevant. If you're not nice to me, brother, I may just sell the lie that he's a talking king penguin. Or a lopsided minihumbug. Ooh, or maybe even a jelly doughnut that just *thinks* he's a boy. Then where would he be? There aren't many parents who would let their children play with a deluded jelly doughnut."

"You wouldn't dare," said the Facttracker.

Ersatz looked him straight in the eyes and snapped his fingers again. Before the Facttracker even knew what was happening, a large hole opened in the floor beneath him, the lions released their grip, and he vanished into the darkness below.

"Wouldn't I?" Ersatz said flatly.

He then turned his attention to the terrified just small enough boy. Eyes wide with focus, Ersatz examined him carefully, looking him up and down and smiling all along.

"Yes," said Ersatz, "oh, yes! A perfectly clean slate! Why, the possibilities are infinite!"

"What are you going to do to me?" asked the just small enough boy with a shudder.

"*To* you?" Ersatz laughed. "No, I'm going to do something *for* you. I'm about to give you an incredible gift, young man. Why? Well, partly because you've been such a help to me—pulling the lever and all—and partly because I just love a creative challenge." He knelt so that he was face-to-face with the just small enough boy. "I want you to tell me what you want more than *anything.*"

The just small enough boy tried to speak but couldn't get the words out.

"You want to know who you are, don't you?" said Ersatz knowingly, and the just small enough boy nodded silently. "Well, I can help you. I can make you *anyone* you want to be."

"No, you can't." The just small enough boy frowned. "No one can. My facts are gone."

"And that's the best thing that ever happened to you!" said Ersatz. "Who you were or were supposed to be was probably dull anyway. Believe me, if you knew who you really were, you'd be bored out of your mind. And that's not a slight against you. *Everyone*'s boring! That's why we have lies." The just small enough boy's resolve showed a hint of wavering, and Ersatz moved in closer. "You're still thinking you're your facts, aren't you? Forget them! *They* abandoned *you*, didn't they?"

"I guess so," said the just small enough boy.

"So why not try lies?" asked Ersatz. "The sky's the limit! Actually, it's not! There *is* no limit! Let's see now, how about Milo Alexander: Polar Bear

Wrestler and Dinosaur Tamer? You like that one, don't you? Yes, I can always tell. How about this one then? David Marinoff: Discoverer of the Subcontinental Ocean! Oooh, what about Buster Chow: King of the Bee People!"

"But it—it wouldn't be real," protested the just small enough boy.

"It would be as real as you believe it to be," Ersatz assured him. "And if it's real to you, it's real to everyone else. Your facts are gone, son; that's the truth. They're gone, and they're never coming back. But I'm offering you something even better. I'm offering you 'You,' the way *you* want you to be!"

The just small enough boy knew that he should run away. But somehow he couldn't. The temptation was just too strong. From somewhere in the distance he heard a voice yell, "Don't listen to him!" But it was too late.

"Could I—could I just be a regular little boy?" asked the just small enough boy quietly. "A regular little boy named Bobby?"

And that was the last thing he remembered.

CHAPTER 22

A Horrible Ending

THE JUST SMALL ENOUGH boy ran out of the Liebrary as fast as he could. He was terribly excited about his new identity and couldn't wait to share it with the rest of the townspeople. Sure, they had been nasty and miserable to him over the years. But wasn't that because they didn't know anything about him? It's extremely easy to be nasty and miserable to people you don't know.

"Hey! Everyone!" he shouted as he ran toward the crowd that was still gathered around the lions. "Guess what? I've got a name! I'm Bobby! Isn't that great?"

But before he could find out what they thought,

something so ghastly and gruesome occurred that it's hard for me even to say it aloud, let alone write it.

A caravan of elephant-pulled Gypsy pirates that had been hopping all around the country with swamis looking for a snail watchers' convention suddenly came speeding through town. As it passed by, the ship's anchor accidentally dragged too close to the just small enough boy, latching on to him and whisking him out of Traäkerfaxx forever.

He was never heard from again, except once by a couple in China, who saw him pass by their tea bag factory.

THE END

CHAPTER 23

A Deeply Heartfelt Apology

I AM VERY SORRY for that last chapter.

That's not at all what happened to the just small enough boy. A caravan of elephant-pulled Gypsy pirates that had been hopping all around the country with swamis looking for a snail watchers' convention *didn't* come speeding into town and he *didn't* get swept up by the ship's anchor. Nothing could be further from the truth; the just small enough boy is fine.

In fact, at the moment he's quite happy.

Why did I write it then? Well, to illustrate a point. If you believed what you read, even for a *second*, even for a *fraction* of a second, then you'll understand just how quickly lies can work. And if they can work that quickly on *you*, a clever, intelligent, sharp individual, well then, what chance could the just small enough boy have?

I'm glad you understand his situation a little bit better now. So let's just forget about the whole thing and agree never to speak of it again. And I promise, I'll never lie to you again.

Ah, but surely you must be saying, "Hey! Isn't this entire story a work of fiction and therefore one big lie?"

Perhaps. But we already agreed never to speak of it again.

CHAPTER 24

Pop Quiz

POP QUIZ! What's the population of Nebraska? If you said one million nine hundred ninety-nine thousand nine hundred ninety-eight, you're wrong. It's two million and six. A group of eight salesmen just moved there. They're testing out a new product called an octocycle. It's a motorcycle built for eight. It goes

really fast, but only seven out of the eight people can steer it. The eighth person is only there to yell *yeeee-haaaa!* whenever they hit a big bump. So far they seem to be having a fine time there.

CHAPTER 25

*What Happened to the Facttracker After
He Fell Through the Hole*

THE FACTTRACKER PLUMMETED through the darkness for what seemed like a long time but was really only a pretty long time. Finally he landed with a series of jolting bounces on a great rope net.

He looked up but couldn't see anything except a dim ray of light from where the hole had originally opened. Pointing his ears upward, he could just barely hear Ersatz talking to the just small enough boy but couldn't make out what they were saying.

"Don't listen to him!" he shouted, but had no idea if anyone could hear him and for the next several seconds was surrounded by the echoing "him . . . im . . . im . . ."

The Facttracker tried to feel his way along the wall, but it only led him back to where he started. He tried climbing the walls, but they were polished smooth and impossible to grip. He tried willing himself out of the hole with his mind, but that never works. He sighed in despair.

And then he heard Ersatz giggling, followed by footsteps approaching the top of the pit.

The Facttracker shouted into the air, "Where am I? What have you done?"

"You're under the Liebrary," said Ersatz, peeking over the side. "Like it?"

"No!"

"What if I told you King Louis the Fourteenth lived quite happily down there for most of his life?"

"Still no! And he lived in Versailles!"

"That's your problem," said Ersatz, lying down and leaning over the side, "no imagination."

"Imagination has nothing to do with it, Ersatz! The reality is I'm stuck in a hole!"

"See? And that's why you'll remain stuck in a hole. If it were me down there, I'd be a million miles away already."

"That makes no sense!"

Ersatz stood up and began circling the top of the pit, his hands clasped thoughtfully behind his back.

"You know, after Father dismissed me," he said, "I didn't know what to do with myself. I mean, what's an unrepentant liar supposed to do?" There was a long silence, and then he continued. "That wasn't a rhetorical question. I honestly want to know. What's a liar supposed to do?"

"I have no idea." The Facttracker sulked.

"My point exactly!" said Ersatz excitedly. "Here I was, a young man with a great talent—a gift, if you will—for lying, and nowhere to apply it. Not around here anyway. So you know what I did? I wandered. I went wherever the five winds would take me. And as I'm sure you're aware, the five winds go everywhere."

"There are only four winds, Ersatz."

"Not today, brother, not today," said Ersatz happily. "But I digress. Wherever I found myself, I would look around. And do you know what I discovered? Lies are everywhere. I mean it—*everywhere*! From the smallest small town to the biggest big city, wherever there are people, there are lies. But you'd never know it by asking thcm. No, people never admit that they tell any lies. But they do! All of them! And do you know why they tell lies? To keep the misery away. So I asked myself: 'What's causing all this misery?' And do you know what I discovered? It was the facts. The facts made them unhappy. The facts about the world, about their lives, about themselves. And yet they persisted in calling facts good and lies bad. Why would any sensible person do that?"

"Because it's right," interrupted the Facttracker.

"*That* question actually *was* rhetorical," interrupted Ersatz. "But no, that's not why. They do it because no one ever told them it was okay not to. The problem with lies isn't that they're bad; it's that they've got bad publicity. What they needed was a spokesman, a salesman. And now they've got the best one around—from Azwerp to Zelslow!"

"There's no such place as Azwerp! Or Zelslow!"

"Not yet," replied Ersatz. "But the world is changing quickly. Why, just yesterday Traäkerfaxx was a facttracking town. Now it produces lies. Perhaps tomorrow there'll be an Azwerp and a Zelslow. Perhaps they'll be the same place."

"They can't *both* be the same place, Ersatz! The simple rules of time and space dictate that—"

"You *still* don't get it," said Ersatz. "There *aren't*

any more rules. Anything's possible now!"

"They're just lies, Ersatz. There's no truth to them. They don't *actually* change anything."

"On the contrary, brother, they change *everything*. And when the Liebrary produces its billionth lie . . . the world will be *permanently* changed."

"That's not true! No matter how many lies people buy it won't change anything, Ersatz! The world can always be restored!" shouted the Facttracker into the darkness.

"*Now* who's lying, brother?" And Ersatz smiled as he sealed up the hole and walked away.

CHAPTER 26

The Facttracker's Convoluted Conversation
with No One

"**W**ELL, THIS STINKS!**"** exclaimed the Facttracker, not so much in anger as in observation. It was true, it did stink in there. Like a rosebush that somehow sprouted old sneakers instead of roses.

"Zero is the biggest number," said a voice.

The Facttracker spun around, searching blindly in the darkness.

"Uh, hello?" he called out. "Is—is someone there?"

"No. There's no one there," said another voice.

"Who said that?"

"No one said it," said yet another voice.

"*Someone* must have said it," said the Facttracker.

"Things are said all the time without anyone's saying them," said even another voice.

"That makes no sense," replied the Facttracker, beginning to get frustrated.

"Things that make no sense make perfect sense," said a different voice.

"No, they don't!" huffed the Facttracker. "Where are you getting your information from? You're very ill informed, whoever you are."

"The largest mammal in the world is the tangerine."

"The largest mammal is the blue whale!" shouted the Facttracker. "And tangerines aren't mammals!"

"Grasshoppers are mammals."

"No! Grasshoppers are insects!"

"Tangerines are insects."

"Tangerines are fruit!"

"Blue whales are the biggest tangerines."

"Arrgh! Are you even *thinking* about what you're saying?" shouted the Facttracker, hopping up and down on the net in frustration. "I don't understand this! Who are you? Where am I?"

As the Facttracker jumped on the net, he

looked down. What he saw made him not only stop jumping but freeze in mortal terror. Below the net, in a swirling swarm of twisting tangles, were thousands upon thousands of lies.

And then, to his utter horror, the Facttracker understood exactly where he was. He was suspended above the original hole that Ersatz had dug, which had grown into a mighty pit. A pit for creating and containing the Liebrary's countless lies. And at the very bottom of the pit, glowing faintly from beneath all those lies?

The seed of truth.

"Well, this stinks!" grumbled the Facttracker, this time in anger.

"No, it smells great in here," replied a lie.

CHAPTER 27

A Day in the Life of Bobby

IT WAS A SENSATION unlike any other. A feeling of acceptance, of belonging. For the first time in his life the just small enough boy knew who he was. He was Bobby.

And Bobby was one heck of a kid!

He was four feet five inches tall, liked going to baseball games, and loved playing with big fuzzy dogs. He had a kid sister named Nicole and two parents who loved him dearly; their names were Richard and Judy. They all lived together in a large but not ostentatious house in a quiet but not snobbish community. His favorite color was azure, his favorite food was lobster with butter, and he had a tiny scar on his left knee from when he fell off a skateboard.

Life was great. He was great! *Lies were great!*

Suddenly the mayor skipped by. He was wearing his underwear and socks and nothing else. "I'm a skinny man!" He giggled as he passed. "Skinny and smart! Skinny and smart!"

"And I'm Bobby!" The just small enough boy giggled right back at him.

"Cool!" said the mayor. "Well, come on, Bobby!"

"Okay! Where are we going?" said the just small enough boy, barely able to contain his glee.

"To go get more lies from the lions!" cried the mayor. "Come join me!"

The just small enough boy smiled with bliss and skipped off happily with the mayor. First he got an identity, and now he was being treated as an equal; this was quickly turning into the greatest day of his life.

A few skips later they were at the front of the Liebrary with the rest of the townspeople. They arrived just in time to see a man with a twitchy hand putting the finishing touches on the new town sign, which read in squiggly, drippy letters:

TRAÄKERFAXX: A SWELL PLACE TO BUY LIES!
ALSO HOME OF THE WORLD-FAMOUS MAN-EATING
BULLFROG
AS WELL AS FIVE OF THE SEVEN WONDERS
OF THE WORLD,
TWO AND A HALF OF THE THREE MUSKETEERS,
AND BIGFOOT

The just small enough boy couldn't believe his eyes. There were lies everywhere. In the short time that he had been inside the Liebrary the lions had spewed out hundreds of them, and the townspeople were running every which way, bragging about their fabulous new lies. The mayor cleared his throat, and everyone stopped and looked over.

"Everyone, this is Bobby," said the mayor, putting an arm on the just small enough boy's shoulder and introducing him to the townspeople. "He used to be that kid we didn't know anything about."

"Hiya, Bobby! I'm an excellent singer! La-la-la-*loo*!" sang a tone-deaf man.

"Try not to be too jealous, Bobby. My purple dress is the most beautiful in town," said a woman in a raggedy white dress.

"I'd shake your hand, Bobby, but I don't want to accidentally crush it since I'm as strong as ten grizzly bears! Grrrrr!" growled a scrawny ninety-eight-pound man.

Bobby was thrilled. The townspeople were thrilled. Everyone was completely, utterly thrilled. It had been less than twenty-four hours since Ersatz's arrival, and they were all settling perfectly into their new industry.

"Come gather! Come gather!" cried the lions as the townspeople crowded around them.

"Who wants a lie about Antarctica, the hottest place on earth?" asked the first lion.

"Ooh! Ooh! I do! I do!" shouted a woman with one blue eye and one green eye. As she grabbed it, the lie squeaked, "Antarctica is the hottest place on earth," and she stuffed it in her purse.

"And who wants one about how beautiful land-fills are?" asked the second lion.

"Me, me, me!" cried a man who once got in trouble for putting a thumbtack on his best friend's chair.

"Let's see now, I have a lovely lie about how articulate the mayor is," said the first lion.

"Gimme! Gimme! Gimme! Gimme! Gimme!" begged the mayor.

The lion held the lie out, and the just small enough boy stepped forward to fetch it for the mayor.

"No, no," said the mayor, laying a hand on his shoulder. "You don't have to do that, Bobby. I'll get it myself."

And he stepped up to the lion and grabbed the lie himself, which was something the just small enough boy had never seen him do. This was indeed turning into a truly great day.

"Well, my basket's completely full now," said the mayor. "Grab some of your own, Bobby, and follow me."

It was at that very moment that Ersatz reap-peared. He was smiling quite happily and seemed to be silently chuckling about some private joke.

"Where are you going, Mr. Mayor?" asked Ersatz with a bemused look on his face.

"To go sell these lies," answered the mayor.

"Oh, but you can't just send them out like that," said Ersatz. "Lies aren't like facts."

"They're not?"

"Oh, no, no, no. You can't just sell a lie. You have to really *sell* your lie. Do you understand?"

"Not at all," replied the mayor happily.

"Then I'll show you," said Ersatz, positioning himself so that he was facing the mayor. He motioned with his hands, and the townspeople all gathered around in a large semicircle.

"All right, Mr. Mayor. Repeat after me," he said. *"'No, seriously, Henry the Eighth invented the bicycle.'"*

"Henry the Eighth invented the bicycle," said the mayor.

"Very good!" exclaimed Ersatz. "But don't forget the 'no, seriously.' It lets people know you're serious. And if they think you're serious, then they'll think you're telling the truth."

"But I'm not telling the truth," protested the mayor. "I'm lying."

"Yes, but you want people to *think* you're telling the truth," explained Ersatz. "If they think it's the truth, then they believe it, and if they believe it long enough, then it becomes the truth. That's what makes the lie so good." The mayor let out a thoughtful and serious *ooh*, and Ersatz continued. "Now let's try something a little more difficult. Everyone try it, and remember, say it like you mean it: *'I'm telling you, it's totally true, the ancient Egyptians built the Pyramids with Elmer's glue.'*"

The townspeople repeated his line with a great deal of fabricated seriousness in their voices.

"Excellent! See how much better it sounds when you sound like you know what you're talking about. Now let's try a really complex one: *'My good friend Tony, a renowned history expert, says the world was created last Tuesday, by a guy named Maurice.'*"

The townspeople repeated it.

"Outstanding!" cheered Ersatz. "You see, this one works because your fictitious friend Tony serves as the reliable source. And since Tony doesn't actually exist, he can't possibly refute your claim. So unless someone's willing to do the research, which ninety-nine percent of the time they won't, you're totally safe."

"What about the other one percent of the

time?" asked the mayor.

"Ah, good question. Then you simply tell the truth."

"The truth? But aren't we trying to sell lies?" asked the mayor.

Ersatz took a deep breath and paused for dramatic effect. He looked over the crowd and smiled curiously. "The greatest skill a liar can have," he said slowly and deliberately, "is to be able to tell the truth sometimes."

"Oo-ohh," exhaled the mayor. Behind him, the crowd nodded in silent appreciation.

"Okay! Good job, everyone!" said Ersatz, clapping his hands. "Now let's get some lunch and then go sell these lies!"

"Lunch?" The mayor giggled, hopping up and down excitedly. "I love lunch! What are we having?"

"Why, the healthiest thing in the world, of course," answered Ersatz. "Candy!"

CHAPTER 28

Candy Is Dandy, but Lies Are Unwise

"TO THE CANDY SHOP!" shouted the mayor, and he sprinted off, the townspeople following close behind. The mayor was the first to arrive at the shop, and he immediately flung open the door. With a squeal of delight he hungrily leaped into a barrel of candy, and the townspeople quickly followed suit, knocking barrel upon barrel of candy onto the floor until the whole place was awash with spilled sweets.

"I love candy!" cried the just small enough boy as he bit into a hunk of taffy.

"Of course you do, Bobby," the mayor assured him, cramming a mammoth lolly into his maw and climbing up onto the main counter to survey the penny candy plunder. *"Everyone* loves candy! Here's a little trick I learned: If you empty your pockets, you can stuff them full of candy. Then you have candy in your pockets whenever you reach into your pockets to get anything."

"Um, you don't have any pants on," noted the just small enough boy.

"Yes, but fortunately I had pockets sewn onto all my underwear years ago in case of just such an event," explained the mayor. "My tailor said I would never need them. *Pfft.* What did he know!" And he stuffed a fistful of licorice into his underwear pocket and dived off the counter, cannonballing into a mound of marshmallows to the excited cheers of the townspeople.

"Jump on in, Bobby!" shouted the mayor when his head finally emerged from the marshmallows. "It's like being in the stomach of a whale, if whales ate marshmallows instead of whatever it is that they do eat."

"Watermelons, Mr. Mayor," chirped Ersatz from the back of the room, where he was lazily lounging on a pile of cotton candy, smiling happily to himself.

"Oh yes, well, that makes sense. They live in

the water," said the mayor. "Now jump in, Bobby! Jump, Bobby! Jump!"

The townspeople quickly joined in, cheering him on in festive voices, and soon the whole room was chanting, "Bob-by! Bob-by! BOB-BY!"

Overcome with a joyous, carefree glee he had never even imagined before, the just small enough boy shouted, "I love lies!" and dived off the counter into a hill of caramels. He emerged from the caramels with a sugary smile across his face. The mayor sauntered over and gave him a genial nudge.

"I like this version of you much better, Bobby. The old you was always walking around looking for yourself. It gets old after a while, you know?"

"Yeah, I know," agreed the just small enough boy quietly.

"Now you seem so"—the mayor paused, struggling for the right word—"knowable. You're like a real little knowable person now."

"Thank you."

"You should have gotten yourself some lies years ago, Bobby," said the mayor. "I can tell we're going to be great friends from now on, Bobby: You, all knowable, like you are, and me, all skinny and smart, like I am. Did I tell you that I'm skinny and smart?"

"Yeah, you mentioned that earlier. Congratulations," said the just small enough boy.

The mayor smiled proudly and then stopped, felt around his mouth with his tongue, and plucked some taffy out of his teeth with a string of licorice.

"Y'know, my parents always used to say that too much candy would rot my teeth and make me get fat," said the mayor, his eyes wide with excitement as he crammed a chocolate bunny into his mouth. "*Pfft*. What did they know? Look at me, I'm waist deep in candy and as skinny as ever! And smart too!"

The just small enough boy suddenly remembered that Ersatz's lie had also given him parents, parents who would be at home waiting for him.

"Oh, my God! I have to go!" said the just small enough boy, who couldn't believe that he hadn't gone home immediately.

"I'll see you later on at the Liebrary," said the mayor. "We'll get some lies about that outfit you're wearing." And he turned around and ran back into the crowd, where he belly flopped into a pool of pralines. As the just small enough boy walked out of the candy shop, he could hear the crowd cheer excitedly and the mayor shout out, "I'm skinny and smart!"

Walking along the winding cobblestone streets of Traäkerfaxx, the just small enough boy marveled at the town. Of course he'd done this same walk thousands of times before, but somehow this time it seemed completely different. Before, he'd spent almost all his energy searching the ground in the vain hope of spotting his facts. But now those facts didn't matter anymore, and he was free to simply enjoy the peace and tranquillity of the walk itself.

The first stretch of the walk was a giddy amble as the just small enough boy laughed quietly to himself, thinking about how great the lie was that he had parents. The more he thought about the lie, the more it grew and shaped in his head. And the more it grew, the more he believed it. He spent the next several minutes lost in a cloud of what-ifs. *What if my parents are movie stars? What if they're international secret agents? Or Olympic athletes? Ooh, what if they're famous international movie star Olympic secret agents waiting for me to come home so they can take me to the biggest amusement park in the world? The biggest amusement park in the world . . . on the moon!*

Soon the lie was so rooted in his mind that he

could actually picture his parents waiting in their living room for him. His father was a striking man in an eccentric yet somehow dignified purple tuxedo, who was looking out the window for him through a pair of supersecret binoculars while absentmindedly polishing the two dozen gold medals around his neck. His mother was a brilliant-looking woman in a ball gown and jet-pack, who was cheerily spelling Bobby's name on a world-record-winning apple pie she had cooked for him. It was a warm, loving home filled with two people who loved him.

Spurred on by the escalating awesomeness of the lie, the just small enough boy raced home. He felt a whirlwind at his back as he rounded the corner of Fact Sheet Street and skipped up to his house, which was no longer a doghouse but a stately abode.

"Mom! Dad!" he cried as he reached for the door. "It's me, Bobby! I'm home!"

The second his hand touched the doorknob he regretted it.

Like a curtain coming down on a great play, the fantasy of being Bobby was pushed aside by the reality of what lay behind the door. There was no mom. There was no dad. There was no warm, loving home filled with the people who loved him. There was only a small, cold, empty doghouse.

Have you ever had a dream that was so amazing that you wished it would go on forever but that just when it's at its best moment someone taps you on the shoulder? What do you do? You resist. You try to go back to sleep. You struggle to eke out every last moment of the dream before you have to open your eyes and resume your real life.

Well, that's exactly what the just small enough boy was doing. And to be perfectly honest, so amazing was the dream he'd been having that he probably *could* have gone back to sleep. But then he saw something that washed the dream away forever: the walls of the doghouse. Not the walls themselves, of course, but what covered them: the thousands of facts about his parents.

As he read them, the just small enough boy suddenly saw the lie for what it was: just a big lie. He *had* parents, real parents, and though it was painful to accept the truth that they were missing, even the love of missing parents is still more satisfying than the illusion of fake parents. Being Bobby no longer felt great. It didn't even feel good. It just seemed ridiculous and pathetic and utterly empty. The just small enough boy was furious at himself for ever believing in it. He wondered what the Facttracker would say when he heard.

And then he remembered about the Facttracker.

The just small enough boy ran over to the Liebrary's entrance as fast as he could. He tugged at the door and pounded on it with his fists, but it was no use; it was sealed up tight. He thought about calling the Facttracker's name but then reconsidered. If Ersatz heard him, he'd know that the lie had worn off. Plus there was no guarantee that the Facttracker was still down there. In fact, there was no guarantee that the Facttracker was even still alive.

This was rapidly turning into the worst day ever.

And then the just small enough boy had a thought. Looking around to make sure no one was there, he reached deep into his pocket and pulled out the veriscope. It was in a pretty sorry state; nearly all the branches were snapped off. All but *one*, a tiny branch right in the middle.

"Well, it's worth a try," he said, and put the veriscope up to his eye.

The damaged veriscope hissed and popped as the shadows of translucent images began to appear in its lens. The translucent images grew into wispy letters, and the wispy letters grew into blurry words.

But sadly, that's as far as they got. The veriscope simply lacked the strength to perceive anything with clarity.

"Come on, veriscope! Help me out here! I'm trying to find the Facttracker!" he pleaded, pointing it all around. But no matter where he pointed the veriscope all he got were blurry, fuzzy, illegible words.

The just small enough boy groaned in pain. His eyes hurt, and his brain was numb with frustration. He wished the Facttracker were there to help him but then realized that if the Facttracker were there, he wouldn't even need to be doing this in the first place since what he was trying to do was find the Facttracker.

And then something peculiar happened. As he was looking around, he accidentally caught a glimpse of himself in the Liebrary's reflective stone. Through the lens, he saw two just clear enough facts hovering around his reflection. The first, which he knew already, was that he was neither too small nor not small enough. But it was the second fact that caught his attention: *What you are looking for is in Nebraska.*

CHAPTER 29

Nebraska? How Is He Going to Get to Nebraska?

THE JUST SMALL ENOUGH boy had no idea how to get to Nebraska.

This was, of course, perfectly understandable since he had spent his entire conscious life in Traäkerfaxx. Nevertheless, it did make the journey there a tad more complicated.

After a few moments of considering his options, he decided that his best bet was to try the train. So he headed off to the Traäkerfaxx train station on the outskirts of town.

The station was located in a large glass dome that stretched over a line of tracks. A long red train sat motionless on the track, huffing quietly and spewing a cloud of dark gray exhaust into the air. People were everywhere; apparently word had already spread about the lies, and curious shoppers were arriving by the dozen.

Of course train rides aren't free, and the just small enough boy had not a penny to his non-name. And so as he made his way through the bustling throng, he became more and more convinced every second that there was no way he was going to be able to con his way onto the train.

Amazingly, when he finally did manage to think of a plan, it was so brilliantly clever and masterfully crafty that you wouldn't believe it even if I told you. So I won't. Instead I'll skip right to what happened once he was on the train, which was, in and of itself, a somewhat unbelievable thing.

Right before they departed, the train conductor, a sweet and kindly woman, noticed him standing at the back of the train.

"Aww. You just have a seat right there, young man," she said, guiding the just small enough boy to an empty seat, "and we'll be in Nebraska in no time. And if you keep looking out that window, you might even catch a glimpse of an iceberg or two."

"An iceberg?" asked the just small enough boy. "There aren't any icebergs in Nebraska."

"No, but there are a ton of them in Alaska!" she shouted jovially. "And I've just discovered that the shortest distance between two points is to make sure the points rhyme, so we'll be spending quite a bit of time in Alaska on our way to Nebraska. Y'know, I've always wanted to see Alaska, but my job simply never allowed it. Now I can!"

The just small enough boy groaned. He hadn't expected the lies to be selling this quickly.

"Cheer up," said the conductor consolingly. "I hear Alaska's known for its beautiful windmills. Maybe if you're lucky, you'll get to see one of those too." And with that, she pushed the throttle to full speed, and they sped off toward Alaska.

Well, as you probably guessed, the train struck an iceberg and sank.

The just small enough boy would surely have been lost if not for the Russian submarine that was passing by. The sailors immediately brought the just small enough boy inside and gave him some hot cocoa.

"Th-thank you," stammered the just small enough boy as he sipped the cocoa and tried to warm up.

"*Da.* You're very lucky little boy," said the captain. "We were just getting out of water when you climb on roof."

"Getting out of the water?" asked the just small enough boy. "Why? Shouldn't submarines stay below the surface?"

"Oh, no." The captain laughed. "*Sub* means 'above.' And of course, *marine* means 'desert.' We're going to the Sahara desert. I hear there's good trout fishing there."

The just small enough boy rolled his eyes. And the next day, when the submarine got stuck in a sand dune, he thanked the sailors for the rescue and the cocoa and headed off again.

Good fortune was with him, and he managed to catch a ride with a passing zeppelin. But after the pilot had decided to replace the hydrogen with buttered popcorn, their voyage slowed down considerably.

Which was why he had to accept the invitation to join the earthbound Society of Overweight Australian Hang Gliders. And then the ill-conceived Union of Jetpacking Pyromaniacs. Then the stationary one-legged Scandinavian unicyclist. Followed annoyingly by the stickless Canadian pogo stick team. And then the pointless

Panamanian snowshoeing quintuplets. The list went on and on, but each time the just small enough boy thought he was finally headed to Nebraska, the lies threw him off course again. By his own calculations, he had crossed the globe three times already and was no closer to Nebraska than when he had started.

He couldn't believe how fast the lies had spread. It seemed impossible to him, but the lies were already in every country and every language. When he was in Traäkerfaxx, all he had worried about was getting his facts back and helping the Facttracker. Now he was starting to worry that it wasn't just Traäkerfaxx that was in danger. It was the entire world.

The wind howled forebodingly in the distance, and the just small enough boy looked around. He had no idea where on earth he was. This was especially astonishing since the area was covered with road signs of all shapes, sizes, and colors.

A large yellow square sign read:

> *TIMBUKTU–*
> **10,000,000** *MILES*
> *THIS WAY OR THAT.*

To its left, a red triangular sign stated:

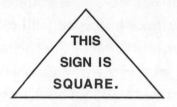

And in front of it, a purple pentagonal sign informed:

The just small enough boy appeared to be standing at a crossroads, but where the roads led was a mystery. In every direction the horizon stretched out, flat and faceless, and the first stars of the evening were beginning to poke out above him.

"Where am I?" he shouted into the oblivion, but only the howling of the wind came as a response.

"What am I supposed to do?" he shouted even louder, but again without reply.

"How do I know which way to go if the signs

don't make any sense?" he screamed so loudly that his voice went hoarse. But there was still no answer. Consumed by despair and exhaustion, he dropped down in the middle of the road.

"I guess it'll just end here," he said to himself as his eyes began to flutter shut. And just as the last dregs of hope were about to slip away, he noticed something.

The North Star.

His brain clicked back to the night of the explosion. He remembered walking through the Factory, reading the handful of facts that the Facttracker had given him. At the time it had felt like the most vivid night ever. Now, just a week later, it seemed like such a distant memory.

But that distant memory had a useful seed at its center: that the North Star makes a perfect point of reference. And he realized at that moment that he wasn't doing this just for himself, and he wasn't doing this just for the Facttracker. He was doing this—this impossible journey—for the seed.

"I may not know where I'll end up," he said, standing up and brushing himself off, "but at least I know which way I'm going."

And he set off again.

CHAPTER 30

The Phony Express

BACK IN TRAÄKERFAXX, business was booming. The lies were being produced faster than ever, and the Traäkerfaxxians were busier than ever. Each morning the townspeople would walk over to the Liebrary, listen to the lions, collect all the lies they could carry, and then go off to sell them. Whom did they sell them to? you ask. Well, anyone they could, which was nearly everyone.

People were coming from all over the globe to get their hands on the world-famous Traäkerfaxx lies. By the middle of the Liebrary's first week there wasn't a single country whose citizens hadn't purchased at least a few useful lies. By week's end most of them were steady customers.

As for the people who couldn't make it to Traäkerfaxx, there was a brand-new delivery service, the Phony Express. Ersatz emptied out the old Traäkerfaxx Fact Sales and Distribution Office and set up shop there, where he created a simple and cost-effective system. The purchased lies were tied to the backs of thousands of snails because as everyone knows, snails are the fastest living creatures on earth. Then Ersatz fed the snails lies about where they needed to migrate. He also fed them the lie that snails *do* migrate.

At first the steady stream of slithering snails was a little disconcerting to the Traäkerfaxxians, but after a while they learned to simply step over it.

And so within nearly no time at all, Traäkerfaxx was a very different place. With all the money they earned from selling lies, the townspeople bought all sorts of things. What sorts of things? Well, *any* sorts of things. They didn't really care. They just liked buying things. Tables, chairs, jewelry, paper, paper clips, candles, candlesticks, elephants, nail clippers, pencils, tugboats, shoes, socks, cups, water towers, licorice

sticks, picture frames, clothespins, five hundred pounds of rice pudding, spoons, eyeglasses, lamps, water beds filled with grape juice instead of water, crepes, ladders, watches, another pound of rice pudding, rope ladders, velvet Elvis paintings, tote bags, peanuts, big furry dogs, pillows, little hairless dogs, fans, pens, scissors, aquariums, a bit more rice pudding, toothpaste, baseballs, ducks—you name it, they bought it.

Soon their houses were stuffed completely full with all their new possessions. So the lions told them simply to build new houses on top of the old ones, and the townspeople happily did. Over and over again. Each day they would wake up, look around their houses, declare that they were still too small, and then build bigger houses on top of the existing ones.

There were small shanties, wooden shacks, log cabins, grass huts, canopy tepees, ranch houses, opera houses, firehouses, doghouses, tree houses, greenhouses, warehouses, beach houses, gingerbread houses, lighthouses, pagodas, igloos, brick colonials, split-levels, adobes, Tudors, ziggurats, and sprawling mansions, to name just a few.

On and on this went, day after day, house on top of house, until Traäkerfaxx was filled with hundreds of columns of houses, endlessly reaching toward the sky and swaying precariously in the gentle wind. It was quite a sight, and no one was more pleased with it than the mayor, whose own column of houses was a foot and a half higher than the next highest house column.

Sure, living in a town filled with enormous house columns took some getting used to, but once you *were* used to it you wondered how you had ever lived without it.

CHAPTER 31

What the Facttracker Was Doing Beneath the Liebrary

ALONE IN HIS subterranean prison the Facttracker was doing the only thing he *could* do, count the lies. Each morning he would wake up, look around to see if there was a way out that he hadn't thought of, have his daily argument with the lies, and finally sit back down and calculate how many lies had been produced that day.

It wasn't easy. Perhaps the hardest thing in the world for a Facttracker is to have to watch tens of thousands of hundreds of millions of lies and not be able to do anything about them. And because there was a steady demand for the lies, they were constantly slithering up the walls around him and out toward whatever exit brought them to the townspeople. But no matter how many times the Facttracker tried, he himself was incapable of scaling the wall.

And no matter how many times he told himself that arguing with lies was pointless and immature, he simply couldn't stop himself.

"Rhode Island is the largest continent."

"Asia is the largest continent!"

"Smoking gives you immortality."

"Smoking gives you cancer!"

"The Facttracker is happy."

"The Facttracker is *miserable*!"

It was very frustrating for him, particularly since whenever he thought that he had made some excellent points and clearly won the debate, the lies refused to admit it.

This was how it went, day after day, week after week, with no end in sight.

Ah, but surely you must be saying, "Waitaminute, what was he eating during all this? A man can't sit around in a pit under a Liebrary for weeks and weeks with nothing to eat!" Well, you're absolutely right. That's why it's especially lucky that the Facttracker had just happened to

171

put a dozen tuna fish sandwiches in his pocket before he started doing the Mexican Hat Dance right before the Factory exploded.

Ah, but surely you must now be saying, "Waitaminute, tuna fish would go bad if you kept it in your pocket for weeks and weeks without refrigerating it."

To that I simply say: You obviously haven't read Professor P. S. Schackman's informative book *How to Keep Tuna Fish in Your Pocket for Weeks and Weeks Without It Going Bad*. I suggest you read it before complaining about the tuna situation again.

CHAPTER 32

A Brief Clipping from
Professor P. S. Schackman's Informative Book
How to Keep Tuna Fish in Your Pocket
for Weeks and Weeks Without It Going Bad

Many of you have asked me, Professor P. S. Schackman, what my secret is to keeping tuna fish in my pocket without it going bad. I can't even count the number of letters I receive each and every day asking me this question. Some of you have even stopped me on the street—in front of my very home—to ask me. Please don't do that. It upsets my cat.

My secret is simple. And I guarantee that if you read my book and follow my patented instructions, you too will be able to carry pounds upon pounds of tuna fish in your pocket, as often as you like, for as long as you like, without the risk or worry of it going bad.

Certainly, mayonnaise can spoil in days, if not hours. But consider this: Plutonium has a half-life of twenty-four thousand years. Am I suggesting you make your tuna fish sandwiches with plutonium? Of course not! That's ridiculous!

Or is it?

Yes, it is. It's completely ridiculous. But just *how* completely ridiculous is it? That will be the subject of chapters 2–77.

Now remember, just because plutonium is the most food-friendly of all the radioactive isotopes doesn't necessarily mean it tastes good. That's why it's important to have the following ingredients handy:

$1/2$ pound chopped celery
1 cup lemon juice
4 pickles (gherkin)
2 cups Ma Saltzberg's Plutonium Tenderizer®
$3/4$ cup sugar

Seems impossible? Well, it is. And yet here I am, happily munching on a tuna fish sandwich I made in 1972. What's my secret?

Well, it works only if you're a fictitious character in a fictitious book. Then the laws of nature don't apply to you. The only problem is that you may occasionally have to blow up to help prove a point. Of course, everyone loves a good explosion, so . . .

[Editor's note: At this point, Professor P. S. Schackman exploded. We suspect it was the plutonium. This brief clipping is all that remains of his informative book.]

CHAPTER 33

Traäkerfaxx Gets Strange . . . er

!?!

THE HOUSE COLUMNS were only the beginning.
As the lions produced more and more lies,
the townspeople made more and more
changes.

One day the mayor complained that all the
candy weight he'd put on made it tiring to walk
around. The lions said the answer was public trans-
portation, a system of catapults placed strategically
around town. It was a bit more work to load, aim,
cock, and fire the catapults, but everyone got to
keep eating their candy, so they were happy.

Another day a woman sneezed in front of the
lions, and they told her that pepper prevents

sneezing. The next day everyone in town happily carried pouches of pepper around their waists.

"I can never find my important papers in the clutter of my houses," complained a man. The lions advised him to take all his papers outside and weight them down.

"That's brilliant," said the man gleefully, "but with what?"

"With dandelion fluff," replied the lions. "One single spore should do it."

A day later the townspeople stored their papers outside with only dandelion spores to keep them from floating away. Since the huge house columns kept all the wind out of town, it worked out quite nicely. So long as no one breathed too hard.

The townspeople built an enormous mountain of sweet potatoes when they found out that sweet potatoes were actually more popular than regular potatoes. They replaced the cobblestones with marshmallows, filled the swimming pools with rice pudding, and covered the cats with dog food. They wore big bright labels with their favorite adverbs on them. They decided that no one named Mitch could wear anything purple, that no one wearing purple could talk to anyone named Mitch . . . the list of changes went on and on!

Ah, but surely you must be saying, "Waitaminute, didn't the townspeople think any of this was strange?" Well, to be perfectly honest, yes, absolutely. No one likes living in a town with that many sweet potatoes. To be even more perfectly honest, it was becoming increasingly difficult to distinguish normal from abnormal. But without an alternative in place of the lies, no one dared complain about them vocally.

Except perhaps for Mitch.

CHAPTER 34

Nebraska

OF COURSE THE JUST small enough boy didn't know any of this information about Traäkerfaxx. He didn't know about the house columns or Mitch, and he certainly hadn't read the last chapter. All he knew was that if the world was as confused as it was, then Traäkerfaxx, the epicenter of the mischief, must be an absolute disaster.

It had been almost three weeks since the just small enough boy left Traäkerfaxx, and he had managed to traverse about forty thousand miles. The journey had been long and dangerous, and along the way he had met countless travelers, many of whom were so amazing that they must certainly rank among the most original and memorable characters in the history of recorded literature. Which is why it's so sad that there's no time to describe them.

For there the just small enough boy stood, on the Nebraska side of the Nebraska state line.

Nebraska was not at all what the just small enough boy imagined, which is not surprising since the just small enough boy had never really imagined Nebraska at all. For one thing, there was corn. Lots and lots of corn. For another thing, there was more corn. Lots and lots of more corn. There was corn as far as he could see. There was even corn beyond where he could see. In fact, with the exception of the sky, there was nothing else that he *could* see.

Except a tree.

The tree was an enormous oak, old and impressive, covered all along the top with mighty green leaves the size of badminton rackets. It seemed odd to the just small enough boy that in the middle of miles and miles of corn stood one lone oak tree. But of course this was Nebraska. What's strange in Traäkerfaxx might be perfectly normal in Nebraska.

But Nebraska or not, the just small enough boy

knew that trees don't talk. And so when a voice suddenly burst forth from the giant oak, the just small enough boy immediately suspected that strangeness was indeed afoot.

It was a withered old voice, and it spoke dusty old words. "Nothin' but corn around here," said the voice. "Corn, corn, corn."

The just small enough boy looked at the oak and thought about how to respond. But then the oak continued talking. "And sky," it said.

There was a pause. "And some dirt," the tree voice added. "And whatever lives in the dirt—bugs and worms and such." There was another pause. The just small enough boy opened his mouth to respond, but the tree spoke again.

"And of course this oak tree," it said, seemingly finished.

Now, the just small enough boy had never encountered a talking tree before. But he imagined, rightly so, that if a tree deigns to speak to you, the polite thing to do is to talk back to it.

"Is there anything else around here?" asked the just small enough boy. "I'm trying to find something, and I don't think any of those things are it."

"Oooh," said the tree voice, perking up. "Sounds interesting. What are you trying to find?"

"I don't know."

"You don't know what you're trying to find?"

"No."

"Do you know anything about it?"

"I know it's what I'm looking for."

"Okay. *Now* we're making some *progress*," said the tree voice, growing excited. "You're trying to find what you're looking for. Makes perfect sense to me."

The just small enough boy decided there and then that trees made terrible conversationalists. "Well, I should be on my way," he said politely. "Nebraska's a very big state, and I have a lot of searching to do." And so saying, the just small enough boy pulled out the veriscope to see if it had any new advice.

Without warning, the branches of the tree shook violently, sending a flurry of leaves hurtling to the ground at an incredibly slow speed. When the just small enough boy looked up again, he could see that the voice he was conversing with came not from the tree but from a man *in* the tree, a very old man with sunken saucer eyes and shriveled bony fingers.

"That veriscope," shouted the man in a wild, ancient voice, "that veriscope—it used to be mine!"

CHAPTER 35

Well, That Was Certainly Unexpected!

Now, THERE ARE SOME people in this world who love math, and so they become mathematicians or physicists. Others, who enjoy words, become novelists or poets. There are even some people who relish the thought of plumbing enough to become plumbing groupies or editors of plumbing magazines. And so when you look at it this way, the idea that the Facttracker's father, who absolutely adored tree climbing, would spend the remainder of his great many years in a giant oak tree in Nebraska doesn't seem all that strange.

And yes, it was the Facttracker's father in the tree.

He had been climbing trees for fifty years, since the day he retired and handed the business over to his son, and had recently moved to Nebraska to climb this one. His white hair was now long and flowing, though there was a great deal of it missing in certain places, primarily on top. Not so for his beard, however, which was full and bushy and would have come down to his feet had he not slung it over his shoulder like a great, white, bushy scarf.

"Who—who are you?" asked the just small enough boy, who actually suspected who the old man was but was far too shocked to believe it without actually hearing it directly from the old man.

"*You've* got the veriscope," said the old man. "You tell me."

The just small enough boy put the damaged veriscope up to his eye. It popped and hissed for a moment, but then responded to the sight of the old man as though to an old friend, tracking his facts cleanly and with ease.

The old man is 104 years old the old man is five feet six inches tall the old man has two sons and no daughters the old man has been climbing trees for fifty years the old man used to live in Traäkerfaxx the old man eats a lot of corn the old man detests

olives but not as much if they have pimentos in them
the old man has a broken heart the old man . . .

The just small enough boy looked up in awe
and disbelief. "You used to be the Facttracker," he
said after some time.

"And you're the just small enough boy," said
the old man, who was now dangling upside down
from a branch.

"How—how did you know that?" asked the just
small enough boy. "How did you know without the
veriscope?"

"When you've tracked facts as long as I have,
you don't need a veriscope. My *eyes* are my
veriscope." And he swung playfully from the
branch, so that his head was now exactly even
with the just small enough boy's head.

The just small enough boy looked the old man
straight in his upside-down eyes. "Then you must
know why I'm here."

"*Pfft*, I'm not a mind reader, kid." The old man
snorted. "I just know what I see."

The just small enough boy stepped up to the
foot of the tree. "I'm here because of your son. I'm
here because of Ersatz."

The old man sighed deeply and seemed to get
even older.

"I knew this day would come," he said. "Tell me what happened."

The just small enough boy told him about the Factory and how the Facttracker had finished it. The old man seemed tremendously pleased by this, and a little tear of joy appeared in the corner of his eye. Then the just small enough boy told him how the Factory had exploded. This seemed to sadden the old man tremendously, and his eyes filled up with tears of sadness. Then he told him about the potatoes and the yam and the seed. By the time he reached the point in the story about the Liebrary, the old man was bawling uncontrollably.

"Oh, this is all my fault!" he wailed. "Where did I go wrong?"

The just small enough boy had no idea what to say. "Um, maybe his name," he suggested. "Didn't it ever occur to you that by naming him *Ersatz* you'd be asking for trouble? I mean, doesn't the word *ersatz* mean 'fake'?"

"I know, I know," said the old man in between sobs. "I thought it would be ironic. Like naming a bald baby Curly!"

"So then you'll help me?" asked the just small enough boy.

"Oh, no," said the old man. "On the contrary, there's nothing we can do. This was inevitable."

"But . . ."

"Sorry, laws of nature," said the old man flatly, and crawled back into the leaves.

The just small enough boy had never felt so let down. His heart sank into his hopes, which crashed into his dreams, which completely buried his spirit.

And then, to his complete shock and amazement, the just small enough boy found himself climbing the tree. The old man let out a terrified *eep!* and quickly scrambled higher. But no matter how many branches the old man climbed, the just small enough boy kept pace with him, grabbing branch after branch until he was face-to-face with the old man on the highest point of the great oak.

"I don't know what you can do," the just small enough boy said, shaking with determination, "but the Facttracker, your son, is the only person who has ever tried to help me. And now he needs my help. He said the world is in danger, and I believe him. I saw it myself. You say the Facttracker and Ersatz are supposed to balance each other out? Well, now there's an imbalance! And unless we do something, the lies are going to take over. The veriscope sent me here. And I'm not leaving until I find out why."

They stared at each other for what seemed like an eternity but was probably only a minute. Finally the old man blinked.

"All right then, listen carefully," he said, licking his dry old lips and rubbing his thin old hands excitedly. "I'm going to tell you everything. I'm going to teach you how to be a facttracker."

CHAPTER 36

How to Be a Facttracker in Two Billion One Hundred Twenty-nine Million Nine Hundred Fifty-eight Thousand Two Hundred Sixty-one Easy Steps

THERE'S ONLY ONE thing more boring than learning how to become a facttracker— that's reading about learning how to become a facttracker.

So I won't bore you with the intricate details.

Suffice it to say that the rest of the week was one big blur to the just small enough boy. First he learned the ins and outs of a veriscope, taking apart and reassembling the surprisingly complex instrument over and over and over again, until his fingers went numb. Then he endured a long and difficult lecture on Fact Theory, which was followed by an even longer and more difficult lecture on Lie Theory. Finally they got to the business of actually tracking facts, slowly and simply at first, but the more the just small enough boy did it, the more he felt his confidence quickly grow.

By the time the sun began to set at the week's end, the just small enough boy was a skilled and practiced facttracker in training.

"I must say, you're a very fast learner. I'm tremendously impressed," said the old man as he adjusted the veriscope and handed it back to the just small enough boy for the thousandth time that day. "Now track me a fact about sharks."

"A shark is the only fish that can blink with both eyes," said the just small enough boy after a few moments of looking through the veriscope.

"Very good. Now track one about cockroaches," demanded the old man.

"They won't eat cucumbers," answered the just small enough boy.

"Excellent. Now one about money."

"There are two hundred ninety-three ways to make change for a dollar."

"Well done. Now surprise me."

"Disney World is bigger than the five smallest countries in the world."

"Interesting. I didn't know that. Now do it again."

"If you could weigh the United States, its center of gravity would be Friend, Nebraska," said the just small enough boy.

"Ooh. Very nice," said the old man, truly surprised. "Not only surprising but symbolic as well."

And then a very serious look came over his face.

"Do you promise to always respect the truth?" he asked the just small enough boy.

The just small enough boy nodded.

There was a moment of tension as neither blinked, and then the old man reached over and took the veriscope from the just small enough boy, spit on it, polished it with his beard, and then handed it back.

"Congratulations," he said with a pleased air of dignity. "You're a facttracker."

The just small enough boy beamed with delight.

"Now I can save Traäkerfaxx from the evil of the lies!" shouted the just small enough boy proudly.

The old man stopped and stared at him.

"What makes you think they're evil?" he asked.

"I heard the Facttracker say they're evil," answered the just small enough boy.

"I'm afraid my son the Facttracker has never truly understood lies. He had a terrible experience with one growing up and has been afraid of them ever since. This, I'm sad to say, has always been his biggest weakness. Lies aren't anything to be feared. Loathed and ignored, maybe. But not feared."

"But they destroy the truth," said the just small enough boy.

"It is entirely possible," the old man explained slowly, "to lie using facts and tell the truth using lies. It's just a matter of how you manipulate them."

"I don't understand."

"There will always be lies, and there will always be liars," said the old man without pause. "The true test of a society isn't how many lies it has; it's how many it believes." He looked the just small enough boy straight in the eyes. "Do you understand that?"

The just small enough boy nodded, and the old man continued.

"There can be no such thing as a fact without the existence of lies to distort them. And no such thing as a lie without facts to disprove them. They're connected. What applies to one applies to the other. Ersatz was able to take the seed of truth because unlike his brother, he understood both facts *and* lies. If you want to take it back, you need to do the same. Any more questions?"

The just small enough boy took a deep breath.

"Do you—do you think I'll ever find my facts?" hc asked.

"Do you think you still need them?" the old man asked right back.

"Of course I do!" answered the just small enough boy. "I only have two facts!"

"And look at how much you've accomplished. You made it all the way from Traäkerfaxx to Nebraska with nothing more than a couple of facts and some determination. What would you do with more facts?"

"I'd let everyone know who I am."

"Don't you see? The problem with Traäkerfaxx isn't that there are *too many* lies; it's that they're listening to them. And the problem with you isn't that you don't have *enough* facts; it's that you're not seeing what you've done with the ones you *do* have. It's not how *many* facts or lies that matters; it's what you *do* with them."

"Well, I still want them," said the just small enough boy.

"Fair enough, they're yours," the old man conceded. "Just remember, *you* make your *facts*, not the other way around." And then his droopy old ears perked up, and he looked to the horizon. "Well, I guess that's it. That's all I can teach you."

The old man turned to the just small enough boy, smiled proudly, and climbed back into the tree. "You have to get back to Traäkerfaxx now," he said, popping out from the foliage at the top.

"'Get back to Traäkerfaxx?'" cried the just small enough boy, as the realization of his situation dawned on him. "How am I supposed to do that? It took me almost three weeks to get here. And that was with a ton of luck! I'll never get all the way back to Traäkerfaxx in time to—"

VRROOOOOOOMMMM!!!!!

"I'll never get back to Traäkerfaxx in—"

VA-VAROOOOOOOOM!

"I say I'll never—"

ROOOM-VA-VAAROOOOOOOM!

"Where is that noise coming—," shouted the just small enough boy. But before he could finish his question, he saw the answer. The noise was coming from a group of eight men riding a strange contraption.

"Excuse me," said one of the men, "would

either of you happen to know how to get to Traäkerfaxx? We're trying to buy some lies about our octocycle."

"Like that it's safe," added one of the others.

"Shh!" said a third.

"Traäkerfaxx? When are you going there?" asked the just small enough boy.

"Let's see," said the first man, counting his fin-

gers, "if we leave . . . hmm, right now . . . we should arrive . . . uh, just before sunset."

"Assuming we don't break down again."

"Shh!"

"Could you take me with you?" the just small enough boy begged.

"Well, the octocycle's built for eight," said the first man pensively, "but it can comfortably fit up to eight and a half."

"Maybe not *comfortably* . . ."

"Shh!"

"Well, anyway, you seem just small enough to fit," said the first man, tossing him a helmet. "Can you shout with delight?"

The just small enough boy smiled a just delighted enough smile. **"Yeee-ha!"** he shouted.

CHAPTER 37

---

*Traäkerfaxx Gets Too Strange,
for the Traäkerfaxxians, at Least*

BACK IN TRAÄKERFAXX, the townspeople were breathing a collective sigh of relief. They had just released the snails, sending the Phony Express lies off to their respective buyers, and that meant their work was over for the day.

The mayor plopped down on the grass like a deflated kickball. "Oh, thank goodness the snails are gone," he said, wheezing. "I don't think I can work for one minute more."

Just then Ersatz appeared from the side of the Liebrary. With a gleeful stride, he walked over to the panting mayor and stood over him.

"Shouldn't you be at home resting up for

tomorrow's parade?" he said.

"I'm too exhausted to go home," huffed the mayor. Then he asked, "*What* parade?"

"Didn't you notice the ticker?"

Everyone looked over at the Liebrary. The sign above the lions read:

THE TRAÄKERFAXX LIEBRARY
OVER 999,998,999 LIES SERVED!

"So?" said the mayor, still unable or unwilling to sit up.

"So!" exclaimed Ersatz, running up the Liebrary steps and throwing his arms up triumphantly. "Tomorrow the billionth lie will be here!"

"So?"

"So tomorrow is the Billionth Lie Parade, of course," replied Ersatz.

"And why are we celebrating the billionth lie?"

"Because once the billionth lie is produced, there will be no going back."

"Never?" The mayor gulped.

"Never ever." Ersatz smiled.

The townspeople looked uneasy for a moment, and there was a bit of mumbling and eye shifting.

"I thought you *liked* parades, Mr. Mayor," prodded Ersatz.

"It's not that, really," began the mayor, "it's the lies and—"

"If you don't like parades, just say so," said Ersatz. "I don't want to force a parade on you, with all its fun and paradey goodness. I was under the impression that this was a parade-friendly town. Honestly. I thought it was. But apparently I was wrong. Apparently this town doesn't like parades at all. So don't worry about it, Mr. Mayor. You just lie there and I'll cancel the parade and we can never have a parade ever again with its balloons and confetti and honoring of the town mayor."

"Well, I do love a good parade," the mayor conceded.

Ersatz smiled sharply. "I know, Mr. Mayor. Everyone does. Now why don't you catapult home and get some rest?" Ersatz suggested.

"I've become too heavy for the catapults," the mayor complained, and the rest of the townspeople nodded in agreement. "I can't get up on them anymore. See?" He tried to climb up onto a catapult, but the effort resulted only in a lot of grunting by the mayor and groaning by the catapult.

"Hmm. Replacing your shoes with slippery eels is a sensible solution," said the first lion, and the sign over him clicked to

OVER 999,999,000 LIES SERVED!

CHAPTER 38

The Facttracker Continues to Debate the Lies, with Predictable Results

S ITTING DOWN THERE in the deep, deep pit under the Liebrary, debating with the lies for weeks and weeks, was terribly exhausting for the Facttracker. Keeping count of them was not only exhausting but thoroughly depressing as well. Not even the tuna fish sandwiches, which were holding out just fine, by the way, could lift his spirits.

"Oh my god," he gasped as he finished tallying the day's lies, "that makes nine hundred ninety-nine million nine hundred ninety-nine thousand lies. Which means we're just a day away from the billionth lie." He could barely utter the next sentence. "Tomorrow this will all be permanent," he said, choking.

"It'll be permanent yesterday," a lie corrected.

"Not now!" shouted the Facttracker to the lies below.

"Now is what happens after later," said a lie.

"I'm not in the mood!" yelled the Facttracker. But after a moment of biting his tongue he finally gave in. "And it's what happens *before* later!"

"You *are* in the mood," said a lie.

"No, I'm not!" he shouted back. "And I'm not having this conversation again."

"It's not a conversation, it's a soliloquy," the lies corrected.

The Facttracker said nothing but simply sat down and scowled.

"All babies are born wearing tuxedos," the lies prodded.

The Facttracker stood up and paced around but kept silent.

"Approximately one-third of a television's parts are edible," the lies nudged.

The Facttracker paced faster, bit his nails feverishly, and let out a desperate high-pitched squeal, but he didn't say anything. There was a long silence, and it seemed as if the lies had finally given up. The Facttracker looked down into the pit. Silence. He brushed himself off and slowly sat back down. Still nothing. It had taken him weeks and weeks to figure out how to beat the lies, but apparently he had finally done it. All he had to do was not engage them. It was that simple. He breathed a sigh of satisfied relief.

"The color yellow was originally called banana," said a lie.

"No! No! No!" screamed the Facttracker. "It's not banana, or lemon, or sunflower, or butter! Yellow is a primary color! It has a wavelength of five hundred sixty-five to five hundred ninety nanometers! If you mix yellow with blue, the resulting secondary color is green! If you mix it with red, you get orange! Yellow is, has always been, and will continue to be . . . *yellow*!"

"The opposite of yellow is good-bye," said a lie.

And the debate resumed.

CHAPTER 39

Yeee-ha!

THE JUST SMALL ENOUGH boy rushed back to Traäkerfaxx to stop the billionth lie.

Now, surely you must be saying, "Hey! Waitaminute! How could he know about the billionth lie? He was with the Traäkerfaxxians when Ersatz told the Facttracker and with the Facttracker's father when Ersatz told the Traäkerfaxxians!"

True. But he knew all about it because he'd read the last chapter.

Now, surely you must be saying, "How could he read the last chapter?! Who showed it to him?"

I did. And I'll be honest, I don't normally

agree with showing characters in books chapters that they're not in. But the just small enough boy was having a hard enough time, and I just couldn't stand to make it any harder.

And so with the knowledge of the billionth lie, the ride back to Traäkerfaxx was a mixed bag of emotions for the just small enough boy. He spent the first leg of it completely elated, barely able to contain his glee over his newfound facttracking skills. As they rocketed down the Nebraska dirt roads, the just small enough boy would point his veriscope around and excitedly scream out facts. "That's the ninety-third bug you've swallowed!" or "We've almost crashed thirty-seven times!" When it came time for him to yeee-ha, he would take a deep gulp of air and belt out an enthusiastic *yeeeeeee-haaaaa!*

But as the trip continued, the novelty of the veriscope wore off, and the reality of what lay ahead seemed more and more daunting. Soon they reached the highway, and with the wind whistling past his ears, the just small enough boy was left alone with his thoughts, mostly terrible, involving horrible scenarios of failure. His yeee-has sounded more like yelps.

The last several hours were a blur to the just

small enough boy. He had been through such a range of emotions that he no longer knew what he was feeling anymore. All he could do was sit there, gently stroke the veriscope with his thumb, and stare blankly at the horizon. His yeee-has, when he could muster them, sounded more like questions than exclamations.

And just when he felt that he could take it no longer, there came over the horizon two things almost at once. First one of the men shouted out, "Look! Traäkerfaxx!" and they all caught their first glimpse of the town, the top of the mayor's towering house column peeking over the horizon. Then another man shouted, "Look! Igloo!" as they realized what the house was. And then, almost before they could take in the oddity of seeing an igloo in the middle of the sky, another man suddenly shouted, "Look! Snails!"

Like an enormous black arrow pointed right at them, the road slowly darkened as the swarm of snails burst from the horizon and crept steadily toward them. The first reaction of the just small enough boy, believing that Ersatz had discovered his plan and sent the snail armada to intercept him, was to cover his face. But as the snails drew closer and closer and still paid no attention to him, he began to reassess the situation.

"What could all these snails be doing?" he asked the octocyclists, who had now pulled over to the side of the road to watch the spectacle. "And what's tied to their backs?"

The answer came not from the octocyclists but from the snails themselves. As the first snail reached them, its dangling cargo cried out, "Hot dogs make excellent guard dogs if you use enough mustard!" A moment later the next snail's shipment exclaimed, "*E* before *i* except after *y*!" Then all the lies spoke up. It was only a confusing whisper at first, but gradually grew to a deafening rumble as the swarm overtook them.

As the snails passed by him in their symphony of lies, it seemed to the just small enough boy that the world would never be right again.

CHAPTER 40

Over Nine Hundred Ninety-nine Million Nine Hundred Ninety-nine Thousand Lies Sold

THE SUN WAS JUST starting to go down in Traäkerfaxx, and most of the townspeople were in their homes at the top of their house columns. And so no one heard the unmistakable sound of the octocycle as it drove through the town and screeched to a halt near the entrance to the field.

"Thanks for the ride!" said the just small enough boy, taking his helmet off and hopping out.

"Oh, you're plenty welcome," said the first man. "Now if you can just tell us where we can find the Liebr—" He stopped right in the middle of his sentence. In fact, none of them was capable of speech as they took their first good look at Traäkerfaxx.

Mounds of papers, covered by tiny dandelion spores, littered the grass. Marshmallow fluff, plastered about the sidewalks, bubbled lazily in the hot sun. There was a strange stench of pepper in the air. A man wearing an adverb tag reading "Ominously" skated past them on eel shoes. A single sweet potato bounced down the side of the sweet potato mountain, rolled across the lawn, and came to a stop by the octocycle.

The men turned to one another and nodded quickly in silent agreement.

"Perhaps we'll just be on our way," said the first man, and they sped off in a panicked **VRAROOOOOM!**

The just small enough boy took a deep breath and steadied himself. As he walked through the vaguely familiar cobblestone streets, he noticed a drab silence, almost a seething calm, all around him, the kind of eerie stillness usually reserved solely for hurricane eyes. The only sound that even came close to breaking the calm was the gentle *whoosh* of the house columns swaying back and forth. But even that only served to give the stillness a sense of rhythm.

The just small enough boy soon found himself leaving the oddness of the streets and entering the oddness of the field. At the center of it, of course, was the Liebrary, with its familiar stone lions on its front steps.

Walking slowly toward the Liebrary, the just small enough boy noticed with horror that the sign above it now read: OVER 999,999,000 LIES SOLD!

"Just remember what the old man taught you," he whispered to himself as he approached the glossy Liebrary steps. The second his foot touched the steps, the lions opened their eyes and greeted him enthusiastically.

"Good afternoon," said the first lion. "And welcome to the Liebrary, where we're always open for business!"

"My, you're a large, hulking lad," said the second.

"Um, thank you," said the just small enough boy.

"That one was a freebie," said the first lion. "Would you like to hear another?"

"Christopher Columbus invented the glow-in-the-dark yo-yo," said the second lion, and they both looked down at the just small enough boy to see his reaction.

"I don't think he liked it," said the first lion.

"Okay, this one you'll love! My name . . . is Albert!" said the second lion.

"Ooh, nice one, Dave!" said the first lion.

"Thank you," said the second lion. "But I don't think the kid liked it."

They both looked down at the just small enough boy, who looked back up and smiled politely.

"No, I, uh, I liked it just fine," the just small enough boy said, trying to maintain his just small enough smile, "but I'm looking for some *specific* lies."

"Well, well," said the first lion, "a man who knows what he wants."

"How marvelous," said the second lion.

"So tell us," said the first lion, "what is it that you're looking for?"

"Someone I know is missing," said the just small enough boy, "and I want some good lies about where he is."

"So who is this friend of yours?" asked the second lion.

"The Facttracker," said the just small enough boy.

"I love it!" exclaimed both lions in unison. But then the first lion added, "Especially since he's dead!"

The just small enough boy gasped in horror

but then caught himself, remembering how the lions worked. A sense of relief washed over him. The Facttracker was still alive; now all he had to do was find him.

"I'm glad to hear that he's dead," said the just small enough boy, trying his best to smile while he said it. "Now do you have any lies about where he is?"

"Ooh, me first, me first," the second lion begged.

"Okay, go ahead," said the first lion.

"He's in Antarctica," said the second lion.

"Yes, and he's also in New York," said the first lion.

212

"He's in Belgium!"

"He's behind that tree!"

"He's in the kitchen with Dinah!"

"He's on the moon!"

"He's nowhere!"

"He's everywhere!"

And just then the second lion stopped, and his eyes went wide.

"Oh, my God!" shouted the second lion, waving his paws around in wild panic. "He's right over there! Look! No, really, look!"

The just small enough boy turned around and looked behind him.

"Gotcha!" said the second lion.

"Nice one, Dave," said the first lion.

"Thanks, Frank," said the second lion.

"Wow, those are really, really, really, just great," said the just small enough boy, trying his best to sound impressed. "But do you have any lies saying that he's still under the Liebrary?"

"Nope."

"Good," said the just small enough boy. "And there's no way he can get out, right?"

"He can get out anytime he likes," said the second lion.

"Just as I thought," mumbled the just small enough boy.

"There are a million ways to get out," said the first lion. "But no way to get in."

"No way at all," the second lion added.

The just small enough boy's eyes lit up. So there *was* a way in.

"How?" he asked excitedly. "How can't anyone get in?"

"Oh," said the first lion, looking up at the setting sun, "sorry, but we're closing now."

"Closing?" protested the just small enough boy.

"But I haven't found the lie I need yet! How can you close? You said you were open for business all the time!"

"We lied," said the first lion.

"Now if you'll excuse us, we need to get some sleep," said the second lion.

"We have a big day tomorrow," said the first lion.

"It's the Billionth Lie Day," added the second lion.

"Come back tomorrow," said the first lion.

"But tomorrow will be too late!" cried the just small enough boy.

"Sorry," said the second lion pleasantly but firmly, "but the Liebrary's closed."

The just small enough boy could tell by their tone of voice that there was no changing their minds. If he was going to find a way into the Liebrary, he'd have to figure out a different way.

"Well, thank you," said the just small enough boy, smiling sadly. "Maybe I'll see you again in the morning."

"It's been a pleasure helping such a huge and towering individual as yourself," said the first lion. "Come back anytime."

"Good night," said the second lion. And then

he did something that caught the just small
enough boy's attention. He yawned. And from
deep down way in the back of the bottom of the
depths of the lion came a very specific and unfor-
gettable smell.

Tuna fish.

CHAPTER 41

That Night

I F YOU WERE TO MOVE to Traäkerfaxx at this very
moment, you would see some pretty unusual
things. You would undoubtedly see about a
hundred huge towers made of dozens upon dozens
of houses, swaying in the night. There's a good
chance you would see a random townsperson cata-
pulting across in the blackness, exclaiming how
unusually unlit an afternoon it was. You would
probably see a whole lot of rice pudding. There's
no way you could miss the mountain of sweet
potatoes.

And if you looked really hard and squinted in
the dark, you might even catch a glimpse of the

just small enough boy tiptoeing through the town with a candle in one hand and a line of rope in the other. And if you were to describe what he did next, it would sound an awful lot like this:

The just small enough boy tiptoed silently through the town until he reached the Liebrary. Looking up, he saw that the two stone lions were soundly asleep. Soundly, but not soundlessly. For as they exhaled each deep breath, they mumbled something. They were lying in their sleep.

"Paris is the capital of Vermont," snored the first lion.

"Noses want to take over the world," snorted the second.

Slowly, and tremendously carefully, the just small enough boy climbed up onto the foot of the first lion. Then, even more slowly and more carefully, he pried open the lion's great stone jaw. Suddenly the lion began trembling, and the just small enough boy, certain that he was discovered, flinched. But he wasn't. Instead the lion merely belched.

The just small enough boy quickly tied his line of rope to the lion's bottom tooth and climbed into the lion's mouth. A moment later he closed the mouth behind him.

What happened next? Well, since this was *your* description of what you'd see if you moved to Traäkerfaxx, I suppose that's all that *you* can tell us. Now that he's out of view, I guess *I'll* have to keep telling the story.

CHAPTER 42

Not Inside the Belly of the Beast

I F YOU THOUGHT that the just small enough boy
was devoured by the lion, I wouldn't blame
you. It seems reasonable. He climbed into the
lion's mouth, the mouth closed; he must have
been eaten. It seems quite obvious.

Had it been a regular lion up there, that would
absolutely have been the case. But giant talking
stone lions are a whole different story. They are
this story. And since you are reading *this* story
and not a *different* story, then it seems obvious
that the just small enough boy wasn't eaten at all.

Instead he silently walked over a wet stone
tongue, past a stone uvula, and then, gripping the

rope, rappelled straight down the lion's stone throat. But rather than landing in the lion's stone belly, as you'd expect, the just small enough boy dropped into the hollow pedestal that the lion was sitting on. It was a tight fit, but there was enough room for him if he stayed on his hands and knees.

At the end of the pedestal was an opening, and the just small enough boy could see the two lion tails wagging in front of it. Using his quietest crawl, he slowly made his way toward them.

As he felt his way along the stone floor, his hand brushed against something distinctly plastic. He picked it up and examined it. It appeared to be an old worn-out tape recorder. Inside it was a tape labeled **"BUSTLING MACHINE SOUNDS/ AWESOME PARTY MIX."** The just small enough boy pushed "play."

BANG! CLANG! CALUMPH! CLANG! BLANG! GALOOMPH!

The tape recorder exploded with the metallic chorus of fabricated turmoil, and all around, the walls shook and vibrated. The just small enough boy yanked the tape out as fast as he could, but it was too late. There was no way on earth that the lions wouldn't hear that.

Just as he feared, he heard the lions begin to stir above him.

"You hear something, Dave?"

"Nope."

"Um, are you just saying that to lie, or did you really not hear anything?"

"Huh. Y'know, I don't even know anymore."

"Yeah, me either. Well, good night."

And that was it. They went back to sleep, and the just small enough boy breathed a sigh of relief. Then another sigh. And then a third. But then he reminded himself that there was no time for sighing.

He quickly crawled to the opening at the end of the pedestal and poked his head out to look around. He was back in the same room he had been in last time, only now he was where Ersatz and the Facttracker had been standing. When he had been there last time, only a few spotlights had been on, dramatically pointing to and illuminating the marvels of the Liebrary. This time *all* the lights were on, and the entirety of the room was visible.

The just small enough boy's jaw dropped.

The spotlights had not illuminated the elaborate fresco on the ceiling; they had projected it! The ceiling was little more than a half-painted white stretch of plaster, and the great stone columns that led up to it were actually hunks of plastic covered by a few spotty bits of marble. In fact, he could now see that the inside was mostly dirt floors and mossy walls supported by rickety wooden beams crisscrossing at uneven intervals. The just small enough boy now only wondered how the Liebrary, far from being the architectural masterpiece he had imagined it to be, managed to keep from collapsing on itself.

About a foot into the room he noticed a strange circular pattern on the floor. The just small enough boy stepped out of the pedestal and knelt down to examine it. Brushing away the dust with his fingers, he began to feel a grooved outline form. Soon he could see that it was a trapdoor.

Grunting and straining with all his might, he pried open the lid. A faint silvery light seeped out. The just small enough boy crept up to the edge of the hole and slowly peeked down.

There, suspended on the net above the lies, was the Facttracker. The just small enough boy leaped with delight.

"Heeelloooooo!" he called down to the Facttracker in a loud whisper.

But the Facttracker hardly noticed him.

"A year is a measurement of time!" said the Facttracker.

"What?" asked the just small enough boy, but before he could get any further, the lies interrupted him.

"There are five seasons in a year," said the lies.

"Oh, you were talking to the lies." The just small enough boy laughed. "I didn't realize that—"

"There are *four* seasons in a year," shouted the

Facttracker, completely ignoring him. "Winter, spring, summer, and fall!"

"Thursday is a season," said the lies.

"Are you listening to—," said the just small enough boy.

"Thursday is a day!" yelled the Facttracker.

"Thursday was named after Cornelius Von Day," said the lies.

"It was named after Thor!" shouted the Facttracker. "And there is no Cornelius Von Day!"

The just small enough boy slid down the rope and landed on the net beside the Facttracker.

"Listen, forget about the lies," he said, tugging on the Facttracker's sleeve.

"No! Wait," said the Facttracker, his eyes wild with manic energy. "I've just made a very important point! I think I'm about to win the debate!"

"Cornelius Von Day flew the first airplane," said the lies.

"The Wright brothers—"

"Stop it!" yelled the just small enough boy, giving the Facttracker's beard a yelp-inducing yank.

"But—but I—I've almost won the debate—," the Facttracker protested weakly.

"You're *never* going to win," said the just small enough boy. "They're never going to hear you. All you're doing is giving them power."

"But what else can I do?"

"Don't listen to them," said the just small enough boy firmly. "Don't even acknowledge them."

"The Wright brothers later wed the Rong sisters, who only married them for their *W*," the lies prodded.

The Facttracker started to respond, but the just small enough boy quickly stopped him.

"But—but . . . they're evil," the Facttracker objected.

"They're not evil," corrected the just small enough boy. "They're just dodgy. And they're dangerous only if you let them be."

"Look, you really don't understand—," said the Facttracker.

"I understand *completely*!" cried the just small enough boy. "'There can be no such thing as a fact without the existence of lies to distort them. And no such thing as a lie without facts to disprove them.'"

"What? How—," sputtered the Facttracker.

"I've been to Nebraska."

"Wait," said the Facttracker, bending down and *really* looking at the just small enough boy for the first time, "you're . . . different." And then, as the Facttracker gave a deep head-clearing sigh, his face lit up. "You found me! How did you find me?"

The just small enough boy told him about his day as Bobby, and the Facttracker nodded sympathetically. Then he told him about the train and the journey to Nebraska, and the Facttracker bit his nails nervously. He told him about the tree and his father and the training, and the Facttracker laughed with joy. By the time he got to the point in the story where he arrived back in town on the octocycle, the Facttracker was jumping up and down on the net, cheering him on excitedly.

"You did all *that?*" the Facttracker marveled, eyes wide with amazement.

"Yeah, that's pretty much how it happened. And now I'm a facttracker. Just like you."

The second the words were out of his mouth he regretted saying them. The just small enough boy could see the Facttracker's mood change instantly. He walked over to the edge of the net, looked down at the seed, and pulled at his long gray beard anxiously.

"There's nothing for a facttracker to do anymore," he said flatly. "This is a world of lies now.

What do we have left to fight with?"

The just small enough boy reached into his pocket and pulled out the veriscope. The Facttracker's jaw dropped.

"My veriscope! You fixed my veriscope!" he cried, dancing all around the net happily.

"But it's nothing without the seed," said the just small enough boy.

The Facttracker took a deep breath. "I know," he said. "But it's all the way at the bottom of the pit. And there are . . . a lot of lies on it." He shuddered deeply.

"There *has* to be a way to get the seed," said the just small enough boy, sitting down on the net to think. "Maybe if I trick the lions into sneezing . . ."

Suddenly the Facttracker looked down at his feet and shouted. The shout was a terrifying sound on its own, but what he was actually saying made it a million times more terrifying: *"BE CAREFUL! THERE ARE LIES ON THE NET!"*

CHAPTER 43

The Lions Wake Up

IT WAS TRUE. A few lies had made their way up the side of the pit and onto the net. The Facttracker squeamishly knocked them off with his foot.

"We're too late!" he cried. "The lions must be waking up already."

Almost on cue, they could hear the first stirrings of the lions above them, followed moments later by some muffled words from Ersatz and then from the mayor. As the Facttracker and the just small enough boy tilted their heads to try to hear what they were saying, two things suddenly happened. First a small lie made its way up the side of the wall and then out the top of the pit. There was a brief pause, and then, about five seconds later, the townspeople shouted out, "Nine hundred ninety-nine million nine hundred ninety-nine thousand . . . and one!"

The just small enough boy and the Facttracker turned to each other.

"We're too late!" cried the Facttracker.

Another lie crept up the side. "Nine hundred ninety-nine million nine hundred ninety-nine thousand . . . and eight!" yelled the townspeople.

"No! There's got to be *something* we can do!" protested the just small enough boy as several more lies left the pit. Suddenly he took the rope and began tying it around his waist. When he was done, he looked up at the Facttracker. "Lower me," he said.

"What?"

"Lower me. I'll grab the seed, and then you can pull me back up."

"But the space between the net is too small. No one could squeeze through it."

"Actually," said the just small enough boy as he wiggled through, "the space isn't too small at all. In fact, it's just small enough. Now lower me."

"Just remember," the Facttracker called out as

he let out some rope, "there are a lot of lies down there. Be careful."

"Nine hundred ninety-nine million nine hundred ninety-nine thousand . . . one hundred twenty-three!"

It was a long way down. Much farther than the just small enough boy would have guessed from the net. The lies slowly crept past him as he continued his descent. Most of them ignored him, but occasionally one or two would turn and say, "Only a thousand miles to go," as they passed.

"Nine hundred ninety-nine million nine hundred ninety-nine thousand . . . four hundred eighty-eight!"

He was within a foot of the seed now.

"That's all the rope we have," shouted the Facttracker. "You'll have to stretch!"

The just small enough boy spread his fingers out as far as they would go. He was still five inches away. He extended his arms all the way out. Three inches. He pulled the rope to the bottom of his ankles. Barely half an inch. A quarter of an inch. A tenth of a hundredth of a millionth of an inch . . .

Just then something peculiar happened. The lies suddenly became aware of what the just small enough boy was up to and just how close he was to achieving it. In an act of final desperation, they accelerated their production to protect their source of life.

The just small enough boy watched in horror as the seed vanished beneath the aggressively growing mass of lies. Even worse, they sped up the rate in which they crept out of the pit. The crowd outside went wild as they saw their final goal approaching faster than ever.

"Nine hundred ninety-nine million nine hundred ninety-nine thousand five hundred twenty . . . nine hundred ninety-nine million nine hundred ninety-nine thousand six hundred eighty . . . nine hundred ninety-nine million nine hundred ninety-nine thousand eight hundred ninety!"

The just small enough boy knew he had no choice. He threw his arms up and grabbed the knot around his ankles. And before the Facttracker even had time to finish yelling, "No!" the knot was untied.

The just small enough boy dived straight down, taking a deep breath and pinching his nose just as his head splashed into the swirling mass of lies. There was a sudden rush of words, as though a thousand people were whispering at once. Here and there a single phrase managed to stand out—"horseradish is made of horses," "April is the coldest month," "eighty percent of mermaids are left-handed"—but for the most part it was like passing through a great, noisy wind tunnel.

The just small enough boy felt blindly along the floor. Lies darted in between his fingers like electrified spaghetti. His eardrums throbbed. His lungs burned for air. At last he felt something small and round at the center of the chaos. He thrust his hand out and plucked it.

And then, as quickly as it had started, it was over. The lies evaporated around him with tiny pathetic squeaks, and he was alone on the floor of the pit with the seed in his palm.

But he had no idea if he was too late.

CHAPTER 44

The Billionth Lie

OUTSIDE THE LIEBRARY the townspeople were beginning to get antsy. They had counted nine hundred ninety-nine lies coming out of the lions' mouths, but the thousandth, which would have been the billionth, had yet to emerge.

The mayor was particularly perturbed, as he was wearing his most formal pair of eels and his feet were quite uncomfortable.

"Ahem, Ersatz," he said with an air of polite pushiness, "how much longer will it be? We've been standing here for almost seven hours."

It had of course been only about five minutes, but ever since the mayor let the lions set his watch, he'd been a bit off time.

"Of course, Mr. Mayor, of course," said Ersatz in his most confident voice. He walked over to the lions and whispered in their ears. "Well?" he said, tapping his foot impatiently.

"Well, what?" said the second lion.

"Where's the billionth lie?" snapped Ersatz.

"I don't know," whispered the second lion sheepishly.

"What do you mean you don't know?" shouted Ersatz.

"Not so loud," pleaded the second lion. "You're embarrassing me."

The mayor stepped forward and inserted himself between them. "Er, is there a problem?" he asked.

"Oh no, Mr. Mayor. No, no, no," said Ersatz quickly.

"No, no, no," repeated the second lion, but then a particularly odd thing happened. The second lion got a quizzical look on his face as he suddenly seemed to notice something in his mouth. "That's weird," he murmured as his tongue felt around. "There's a rope tied to my tooth."

And then his eyes went wide.

"There's someone in my belly!" the second lion cried.

The mayor looked puzzled. But before anyone could say anything, Ersatz threw his arms up and shouted, "Ladies and gentlemen! The billionth lie!"

"Uh, how come he's just saying it and there's no actual lie coming out?" asked the mayor.

"Hooray!" shouted Ersatz over the mayor's question. "Hooray for the billionth lie!"

"No, really!" said the second lion in a panic. "There's someone in my belly! And he's trying to crawl up my throat!"

The townspeople shuffled uneasily. And then something gray and fuzzy poked out of the second lion's mouth.

"Look! A head!" shouted the mayor. "And it's attached to the Facttracker!"

The townspeople gasped.

"Get back in there!" shouted Ersatz, his eyes blazing with fury.

"I will not get back in here," said the Facttracker as he crouched in the lion's whimpering maw. "There won't be any more facttrackers going into this lion, and there won't be any more lies coming out!"

Ersatz began to turn a fierce shade of red. But he quickly stopped himself, took a deep breath, and smiled confidently.

"Don't be a fool," he said calmly. "There's nowhere for you to go."

With all his might the Facttracker stood up straight, prying open the second lion's stone jaw as far as it would go. The lion's eyes went wide, and he let out a terrible gagging sound. Before the townspeople knew what was happening, the just small enough boy leaped out and ran straight through the stunned crowd, a small glowing object in his fist.

"Forget the Facttracker!" shouted Ersatz. "Stop the just small enough boy!"

The just small enough boy heard the Facttracker yell, "Run faster! He's behind you!" and turned around to see Ersatz barreling toward him.

He sprinted forward and scampered onto the scooped-out end of a catapult. Ersatz ran at him, arms outstretched and fingers clenching like pincers. The just small enough boy reached down and grabbed the lever.

BOING-OING-OING!

He launched himself into the air, and the townspeople let out a collective groan. But then . . .

KER-BOING!

Sailing over the town, the just small enough boy looked down to see Ersatz flying right at him.

"Give me that seed, boy!" he shouted menacingly.

The just small enough boy ducked just in time to avoid him and landed, slightly panicked, on another catapult. Ersatz landed on a different catapult. Coincidentally, both catapults pointed at the catapult right beside the Facttracker, who noticed this immediately and cried out encouragingly, "Quickly! You can make it!"

BOING! BOING!

The just small enough boy took an early lead. But then Ersatz narrowed his lanky body out and reduced his wind resistance. The just small enough boy tucked himself into a tight ball and pulled ahead again. Ersatz shed his suit jacket and closed in for the kill. A chill ran down the just small enough boy's spine as he felt Ersatz's fingernails scratch at the bottom of his shoe. It seemed that all was lost when . . .

BLUH-BOINGGG!

The mayor departed his own catapult. It had taken all the townspeople to hoist him up onto it, but now he was soaring toward the just small enough boy at top speed.

"I've got him, Ersatz!" he called out as he rapidly ascended.

"No, Mr. Mayor! Stop!" cried Ersatz.

But there was no stopping. Which was unfortunate since as the mayor drew closer, it became obvious that he was headed more toward Ersatz than toward the just small enough boy.

"Turn back, Mr. Mayor! Turn back!" yelled Ersatz, waving his hands frantically.

The mayor slammed straight into Ersatz, and spun him every which way. One of Ersatz's lanky legs clipped the just small enough boy, knocking the seed out of his hand. The townspeople watched in awe as the mayor, Ersatz, and the just small enough boy all plummeted straight into a rice pudding pool beside the Liebrary.

The seed tumbled through the air. The townspeople and the Facttracker watched in mesmerized awe as it sailed over them and landed, with an unnerving scraping sound, in the second lion's mouth.

"*Gulp,*" said the second lion, swallowing it.

CHAPTER 45

The Billionth Lie for Real

EVERYONE WAITED TO see what would happen next. What happened next was this: The second lion puffed out his cheeks, took a deep breath, and seemed poised to let out a mighty roar. Instead he hiccupped. After a moment he noticed that everyone was staring at him.

"Oh," he said, a little embarrassed, and then cleared his throat. "This is not the billionth lie," he announced, and the billionth lie dripped out of his mouth and landed on the ground unceremoniously.

"Ladies and gentlemen of Traäkerfaxx," declared Ersatz, leaping out of the pool and wiping the rice pudding off his face, "the billionth lie!" And then he quickly said, "For real!"

The townspeople gasped. The mayor blinked bewilderedly. Even the Facttracker could barely comprehend what had just happened. The billionth lie had indeed arrived. The world was permanently changed.

"I win!" sang Ersatz, two-stepping through the crowd gleefully. "I win, I win, I win! We all win! Everyone in Traäkerfaxx. Well, not you, brother, but everyone else."

"Yes, Ersatz," the Facttracker admitted in a broken voice, "you win."

"Oh. I suppose that's it then," said the mayor in an exhausted whisper.

"You don't sound very pleased, Mr. Mayor," Ersatz observed, though he clearly wasn't terribly concerned by it.

"It's just so tiring," the mayor whined, digging rice pudding out of his ears. "I'm not sure how much longer I can keep living like this."

"Then for pete's sake, stop!" shouted a voice from the back. The crowd parted to reveal the just small enough boy, covered in rice pudding but otherwise unharmed.

"Look around you, Mayor," he said. "Is this the life you want?"

"Life?" Ersatz interrupted. "What is life but a lie with an *F* in the middle!"

"I guess," said the mayor tentatively, "I guess I thought that the lies would make my life easier. But all they've done is make it harder and harder. I mean, I like being skinny and smart. But it's just too much work when you're obese and dim-witted."

"The Liebrary has produced the billionth lie, Mr. Mayor," Ersatz reminded him. "And that means that the system is permanent. There is no going back!"

"He's right," said the mayor. "The billionth lie means the system is permanent; that was the rule."

"Did it ever occur to you that he was lying?" yelled the just small enough boy. "Yes, there are a billion lies. So what? Like everything else he's said, it's true only if you believe it. There is *always* going back, Mayor. The true test of a society isn't how many lies it has; it's how many it believes."

Ersatz leaped forward.

"Mr. Mayor," he said, weaving his way through the crowd, "are you seriously listening to this . . . boy? This *just small enough boy*? What could a just small enough boy possibly have to say about anything? I mean, if he were Bobby, that would be one thing. But he's not even Bobby anymore. He's no one! You're not going to listen to no one, are you, Mr. Mayor?"

"Oh, well, I guess that, uh, well, I suppose . . . ," mumbled the mayor.

Suddenly, before he could finish, a sound—a deep, grinding, rolling sound—burst from the horizon. It sounded like a strange amalgam of a hand brushing over some grass and an everlasting burp. The sound grew louder and deeper as whatever was causing it drew closer and closer. And then, as a great shadow washed over the town, the answer finally became clear, though not necessarily explainable.

It was a globe. A colossal, thundering globe, rolling into town like a tumbleweed, only the size of a small moon.

Jaws dropped, the townspeople watched in blinkless silence as the globe continued to rumble forward, getting slower and slower as it approached the hill in the town's center. For a brief moment it seemed as though it were about to simply roll over the lot of them. Then, with a grinding, crunching, groan, it came to a stop.

But not before bumping into the mayor.

CHAPTER 46

What Happened After What Just Happened

PANDEMONIUM. The mayor slid across the grass on his eel shoes and plowed straight into the crowd. *Pow!* Like gigantic billiard balls, the eel-shoed townspeople shot off in every direction. *Ping! Pang! Pla-gloomph!* The other man in the other scarf bumped into Mitch, and Mitch bumped back into the mayor, sending him at top speed in the direction of the road.

The instant his eel shoe touched the marshmallow fluff the eel became embedded in the gooey white topping. But the barefoot mayor continued rocketing straight forward.

245

Until he collided with the sweet potato mountain.

The mountain erupted its tubers, knocking the townspeople to the ground. And then *POP!* The pepper pouches exploded.

Three *ah*s later the townspeople let go with a monstrous *choo*!

Ah, but surely you must be saying, "So what! So a bunch of townspeople sneezed, big deal. Townspeople sneeze every day. That's how the story ends? With a bunch of townspeople sneezing? How anticlimactic! Nothing ever came of a sneeze!"

Well, *one* other thing came of it: It blew one of the dandelion spores right off the papers it was weighting down.

The dandelion floated up and delicately brushed against the first solid object in its path—the top house in the mayor's tower of houses. The column tipped and then toppled over to the left, where it struck the next house column, which tipped and toppled onto the next house column, which tipped and toppled onto the next. On and on the columns fell, like giant dominoes made of houses.

Until finally the last one fell with a town-shattering *ka-blooey* . . . directly on top of the Liebrary.

CHAPTER 47

The Last Gasp

T HE TOWNSPEOPLE, as they had done so many times before, gasped. But this time it was a different kind of gasp. It was a gasp of relief. But it was also partly a gasp of sorrow, because they knew that the Facttracker, the just small enough boy, and Ersatz all were still on the Liebrary steps when the columns fell. And there was a bit of a gasp of uncertainty, since they all knew that for better or worse their town was now permanently changed.

It was a very complex gasp.

When the rubble stopped rolling and all the dust finally settled, the townspeople looked around. The Liebrary was a shattered mess. So was the town. So were the townspeople. Slowly, tentatively, they began picking through the ruins.

"I found someone!" shouted the mayor.

Several townspeople ran over, and together they pulled the Facttracker out of the rubble. He was covered head to toe in a fine white dust and coughing fitfully.

"The boy," he croaked in between coughs, "where's the boy?"

"We don't know yet," answered the mayor.

"Then what are you doing talking to me?" he shouted, and dived back into the debris.

Just then a tremendously peculiar thing happened.

The ground beneath them began to shake violently, and several of the townspeople were knocked to the ground. There was a great thundering *BOOOMM,* and a moment later something burst from the rubble in a cloud of white powder.

A large white paw.

A second paw quickly followed it and then a third and a fourth. Then a fifth, sixth, seventh, and eighth. And then a ninth and a tenth, though technically the last two were hands.

When the dust finally settled, the just small

enough boy was there, majestically standing astride the two stone lions, who proudly carried him on their backs.

The Facttracker ran over to them, smiling spiritedly. "You're alive!" he cried.

"The lions saved me," the just small enough boy laughed.

The townspeople looked at the lions. "The lions?" said the other man in the other scarf. "But they're on Ersatz's side."

"To tell you the truth," said the first lion, "we never really liked Ersatz."

"The only reason he used us was for cheap wordplay," said the second lion. "There's no actual legitimate correlation between lions and duplicity."

And they bowed their heads and shuffled their paws ashamedly. Then the second lion opened his mouth and spit out the seed of truth.

"Where *is* Ersatz?" said the Facttracker, carefully picking up the seed.

The lions shrugged.

"Find him!" boomed the mayor, his face redder and redder with rising anger.

The townspeople spread out and looked around, but the only trace of Ersatz found was his white jacket. The mayor was livid. He stomped around the rubble, kicking over bits and pieces of his former town.

"Turn over every rock! Look under every piece of debris!" he shouted. "I want justice, and I want it now!"

The Facttracker put a gentle hand on his shoulder and stopped him. "There is no justice to be had, Mr. Mayor," said the Facttracker.

"But Ersatz tricked us," protested the mayor.

"Ersatz did what Ersatz does," answered the Facttracker. "It took me a long time to understand that."

"But the town is destroyed," the mayor cried.

"*We* chose to destroy it," said the Facttracker. "We chose to listen to Ersatz."

"Then what do we do?" asked the mayor.

The just small enough boy stepped forward. "We rebuild," he said.

"There's only one problem," said the Facttracker uneasily. "I have the seed of truth, but without any facts to feed it there's no way to begin the process. Facts build off facts."

"Oh God!" choked out the mayor. "We're doomed! Doomed! How will we survive? We have nothing! Nothing at all! Nothing to sell, nothing to eat! Nothing but a useless seed and that enormous globe there."

Everyone turned their attention to the enormous globe.

"What is that thing, anyway?" asked the mayor.

The Facttracker walked over to the globe and examined it carefully. Finally he took out the veriscope and pointed it at the mammoth orb.

"They're . . . facts," he announced, and then with a nervous giggle quickly adjusted the veriscope.

The Facttracker looked up, a look of bemused delight on his face. "I can't believe it," he whispered.

"What?" asked the mayor anxiously. "What is it?"

"It's—it's—"

"Oh please, oh please, what?" the mayor begged.

"It's the just small enough boy's fact bundle."

CHAPTER 48

The Answer to Whether the Facttracker Was Right and Then What That Meant for Everyone

THE FACTTRACKER WAS right. It *was* the just small enough boy's fact bundle. It had traveled across the entire globe and was now back with a vengeance. In fact, the just small enough boy had built up so many new facts during his adventures over the last several weeks that the bundle, which was fairly big to begin with, had become positively *colossal*.

"We have facts again!" shouted the mayor. And he reached a meaty fist out to grab a fact off the fact globe.

The Facttracker slapped his hand away. "No!" he told the mayor. "They're the boy's property!"

"But we can use them—," the mayor protested, but the Facttracker would have none of it.

"They're the boy's facts," said the Facttracker firmly. "I think he's earned them."

Everyone looked over at the just small enough boy. But he hardly noticed it. The just small enough boy was in a state of shock. He was in state of panic. He was in a state of exhilarated, delirious daze.

He staggered over to the globe and stared up at it. "There must be millions of them," he said, trembling.

He wanted them more than anything in the world. More than *anyone* had wanted *anything* in the history of *ever*.

"Go ahead," he said quietly to the Facttracker. "You can have my facts."

"If we use them to rebuild the Factory, you may never know what they are," the Facttracker cautioned them.

"It—it's okay," said the just small enough boy.

"You—you would do that?" The mayor blubbered. "You would do that for us?"

"The world needs them more than I do," said the just small enough boy.

The Facttracker wiped a tear from his eye with

his beard and turned toward the globe. The just small enough boy watched with a mixture of pride and sadness as the Facttracker took the seed of truth and lobbed it into the enormous fact globe. Almost the moment the seed touched it, the globe began to spin around, slowly at first, then faster and faster like an enormous top. And as it spun, it burrowed its way into the earth. Deeper and deeper it delved, until the last bit of it was fully underground. And then it stopped.

"Well, that was mightily unimpressive!" huffed the mayor. "That's all it did, dug a hole? What are we supposed to do now?"

"Wait, Mr. Mayor," said the Facttracker calmly.

"I hate to wait," the mayor groused.

And that's when it happened.

There was a brief shudder. The ground shook beneath them. They heard a deep grumbling sound. And then something popped out of the earth.

A sapling. A tiny copper sapling, to be precise.

It unfurled its tiny copper branches and pointed them around at the townspeople, hungrily taking in everything around it. Then it stopped, stretched with a silent copper yawn and began to grow so quickly and powerfully that the townspeople were knocked over by the sheer force of it all.

Up, up the branches went, until they pierced the clouds high above. And when it was over, the townspeople found themselves looking up at the Factory.

One of the leaves fell off and fluttered to the ground. The mayor picked it up and read it.

"The mayor is portly and dim-witted."

Everyone looked at the mayor for his reaction.

"That's so true!" exclaimed the mayor happily. "This thing *really* knows me!"

And the crowd let out an enthusiastic cheer.

"From now on," declared the mayor majestically, "Traäkerfaxx shall always be a facttracking town!" And then he looked over at the Facttracker and smiled warmly. "And the Facttracker will be able to come and go as he pleases."

The Facttracker smiled at the mayor. "That's wonderful. But I think you're looking at the wrong Facttracker." And he put his arm around the just small enough boy.

"Me?" The just small enough boy gasped. "But how can I run the Factory? I don't even have any facts about myself."

"What you just did," the Facttracker said, holding out the veriscope, "told all of us more about you than all your facts ever could have."

The just small enough boy nervously took the

veriscope and turned toward the Factory. As he made his way up the hill, he heard the cries of the townspeople.

"It's great to have a facttracker again!" shouted the other man in the other scarf.

"It's great to have facts again!" shouted Mitch.

"And let us *never* forget this *important* lesson that we've learned!" shouted a man with an adverb tag that read "Heavy-handedly."

But when the just small enough boy opened the door to the brand-new Factory, he suddenly noticed something odd behind it: two pairs of blinking eyes.

It was the just small enough boy's parents. They were covered in facts, but otherwise in perfect condition. With a smile that was brighter and warmer than a thousand suns crammed into a pizza oven wearing a giant wool sweater, the just small enough boy ran over, and they gave him a just perfect enough hug.

Now, surely you must be saying, "Waitaminute! How could they live for so many years inside the fact globe?"

The answer is simple: peanut butter and jelly sandwiches. Well, peanut butter and jelly *and plutonium* sandwiches, to be precise.

CHAPTER 49

Everyone Loves a Happy Ending

Y ES, EVERYONE LOVES a happy ending. And thankfully, every story has one, provided you know when to end it.

This story ends right here, with the just small enough boy's reunion with his parents. It was the happiest moment of his life, though believe me, from that moment on he had many, many happy moments.

Well, that seems happy enough!

In fact, for a story that began with an explosion, this ended up having a surprising amount of happiness in it. But there are still several facts in particular that would make it even happier. Here they are:

- ☀ That from the newly dedicated Fact-tracker statue in the center of Fact Sheet Street, the Facttracker wished everyone in Traäkerfaxx good luck and set off for Mexico, where he can still be found teaching the best Mexican Hat Dance on either side of the border.

- ☻ That the just small enough boy was never known as the just small enough boy ever again. From that day forward he was known to everyone who knew him—that is, everyone in Traäkerfaxx—as the Just Small Enough Facttracker.

- ◎ And finally, that the Just Small Enough Facttracker, who had spent nearly every moment of his life searching desperately for his facts, now found himself surrounded by more facts than he could have ever imagined.

Ah, but surely you must be saying, "What about his own facts? Did he ever find out who he was?"

As a matter of fact, he did. He found out that

he was a lot of different things. He was a smart boy with a brave heart. He was a much-loved son. And once, as a favor to an old friend, he was a substitute Mexican Hat Dance teacher.

But that's a whole other story for a whole other day.

CHAPTER 50

It Isn't Over? I Thought It Would Be Over.
I Mean. What Else Could Possibly Be Left?
What Else Could There Be to Say? Oh. Yes.
Now I Remember . . . Pop Quiz!

POP QUIZ! What is the population of Nebraska? If you said two million six, you're wrong. It's now two million seven. A well-dressed, dignified elderly gentleman in a perfectly tailored white suit just moved there. Despite his recent arrival, however, he seems to be quite popular, amusing the other Nebraskans with his quirky parlor tricks and magnificent ideas on how to modernize the Nebraska economy. But what everyone seems to like most about him is his smile, his bright white charming smile.